Dear Knausgaard

Beyond Criticism Editions explores the new paths
that criticism might take in the 21st century.

We encourage any kind of formal adventure:
analytical, aphoristic, archival, autobiographical,
citational, confessional, descriptive, dialogical,
dramatic, fantastical, fictive, graphic, historical,
imaginative, ironical, metaphysical, miscellaneous,
mythical, palimpsestic, parasitical, philosophical,
poetical, polemical, political, probational, riddling,
theological, theoretical, ventriloquial.

Our only criterion is that it *discovers*.

The series is curated by Katharine Craik
(Oxford Brookes University) and Simon Palfrey
(Oxford University)

Dear Knausgaard

by Kim Adrian

BOILER HOUSE PRESS
Beyond Criticism Editions

"Between the selfless writer and the selfless reader, literature is shaped."

—*Karl Ove Knausgaard*

Contents

February 20-21, 2019	**5**
March 5, 2019	**15**
March 11, 2019	**21**
March 16, 2019	**25**
March 21, 2019	**33**
March 24, 2019	**39**
April 16, 2019	**43**
April 29, 2019	**51**
May 11, 2019	**59**
May 26, 2019	**63**
May 30, 2019	**71**
June 2, 2019	**77**
June 6, 2019	**83**
June 14, 2019	**89**
June 24, 2019	**93**
June 27, 2019	**97**

July 1, 2019	**105**
July 6, 2019	**111**
July 10, 2019	**117**
July 13-14, 2019	**119**
July 21, 2019	**129**
July 24, 2019	**135**
August 3, 2019	**139**
August 22, 2019	**145**
September 3, 2019	**153**

February 20, 2019

Dear Mr. Knausgaard,

My friend Lisa told me the other day, when we were standing in the children's section of the bookstore she co-owns, that she'd read in a recent interview that you've stopped smoking. I was so relieved to hear this I actually felt a weight lift off me. I guess it was visible because Lisa laughed and gave my shoulder a nudge. Later that same day, another friend, who lives in London and who knows all the local literary gossip, informed me that you've moved to that city from Sweden and have fathered yet another child (your fifth) with your newest wife or lover, whichever. I hope your latest domestic arrangement finds you happy, but as an avid reader of your work, I confess I find it hard to digest these abstracted bits and pieces of your personal life. In fact all the hoopla surrounding your extra-literary activities (hoopla many of my more bookish friends feel I need to know) is for me a tempting but ultimately unwelcome distraction. I prefer to read your work without the fluorescent glare of your public persona shining over it. God knows it's hard enough to keep you, the author, Karl Ove Knausgaard, separate from you, Karl Ove Knausgaard, the narrator and protagonist of *My Struggle*. And not just because you've put every last obstacle in the way of the reader who seeks such a division, but because your face, pleasant as it may be, is plastered all over the FSG paperback editions of *My Struggle*, at least as they've appeared here in the U.S. over the past several years. How annoying I find those covers, which for a while were so boldly displayed in nearly every bookstore I ventured into. Even long before I cracked the spine of Book 1, your rugged, vaguely Christ-like features—long, graying hair, soulful eyes, scraggly beard, dramatic cheekbones—actively repelled me from countless display cases. *Who is that glowering man?* I wondered. *What kind of a writer would allow himself to glower so hammily? Isn't glowering, outside of the most popular art forms (cinema, pop music) outdated, even tacky?* But your public persona clearly thrives on old-school tropes like glowering. Indeed, your entire physical person appears to fulfill every last physiognomic stereotype of the macho male genius. You're a modern-day Hemingway. A Norwegian Nabokov. A Bolaño with bone structure. A Sebald with sex appeal. Of course, it's not your fault you look the way you do, but at the same time you are the one regularly posing for all kinds of photos, and those tropes—which demand some cultivation—emanate from you in these photos like an aura of high-voltage static, a fact FSG knew perfectly well when they decided to stick your face on the covers of those books, which they pumped out just as fast as humanly possible—though when all was said and done, the pace of things wasn't really *that* fast given the gargantuan task you'd set your translators. What a monster you've written. 3,600 pages! And here again the question of ego arises, simply by way of page count.

... continued (2 p.m.)

It's incredibly blustery here today. The wind rises and subsides in audible crescendos and decrescendos. Pine cones and shriveled seed pods fly off the bare branches of the trees in our yard and ping against our roof before scattering noisily down its slope. The sky is no color. It's a little frightening. The entire building seizes up in the strongest of the winds, and at these moments the architecture surrounding me feels like an extension of my own body. It's as if my own spine were at the center of it all. Just a few minutes ago, the electric company called with recorded tips for what to do in case we're hit by one of the many power outages affecting the area, but I hung up before it finished. I'm not sure why.

I'm home alone, as is usually the case during my son's school hours. His school happens to be right next door, which is nice because on less forbidding days I can often hear him running around outside, shouting to his friends during gym class and recess. The sound of Jonah's voice floating over the chain-link fence that separates our yard from the school yard makes me incredibly happy even though, every time I catch it, I mourn the day I no longer will, because I'm built that way, with nostalgia at my core, which is a bad way to be built. Nostalgia, after all, is just a sepia-tinged indulgence. And pre-emptive nostalgia is even worse: a masochistic fantasy—one you, yourself, might call "feminine," as you call so many things you deem mild, weak, or false. But I don't mean to put you on the defensive. I see that, already, I've accused you, only quasi-obliquely, of being hammy, macho, egotistical, and, just now, misogynistic. Honestly, it's not my intent to accuse of you anything. I only want to hash out my experience of reading *My Struggle* with you, because it was just that—an experience, one that changed some important things in my own life and mind. For instance, the act of reading is, for me, different now than it was before I read *My Struggle*. So is writing. Beyond that, how I think about life itself has changed; and by life I mean not only my life, and not only human life or social life, but *all* biological activity, which, as you remind your readers again and again, crawls and seeps and races and squiggles and flows over and in and through the cracks and crevices of everything that does not live but simply exists: material reality, in short. In fact, this aspect of your work—your soft-spoken but relentless metaphysics, a metaphysics obsessed with the *inner* and the *outer*, with the *living* and the *non-living*, with the *open* and the *closed*—is one of the more important gifts I've received from reading *My Struggle*. It's like a puzzle I didn't have before. I play with it all the time.

There are other things I received from reading those books, but they are harder for me to put my finger on.

... continued (February 21)

What did I do all day? Straightened the house. Sent a few emails. Some yoga. It doesn't add up.

I'm supposed to be at a music lesson with my son right now (we take flute class together), but I made the excuse of my vertigo, which really has been bad today, and bowed out. Jonah walked to the lesson alone. He's twelve. It's fine. But

I still get nervous. James, my husband, will pick him up at six. In the meantime, here I sit, in front of my laptop at the dining room table with a small plastic tub of Marcona almonds at one elbow and a glass of bourbon at the other. Ah, the guilty pleasures. The smaller they are, the sweeter they are, don't you think? Like reading—the guiltiest of all!

> "For some perverts the sentence is a *body*."
> —Roland Barthes

Here's my thought: I'm going to tell you, as best I can, the story of how I read *My Struggle*. It's a simple story, but it was difficult for me. Not surprisingly, it's a story that begins in a bookstore. Lisa's.

Lisa co-owns and manages the Brookline Booksmith, just a few blocks from our apartment. But her job is much more than a job to her, it's a kind of calling. Books are her obsession, her religion. I'd go so far as to say that Lisa is a kind of high priestess of reading. She has often described to me, for instance, the beauty of those hours before the store opens, before any employees show up, between five and seven a.m., when she wanders the aisles, alone with the stock. "It's a form of prayer," she once said: shelving new books and re-shelving old ones that have been misplaced, climbing and descending the many hanging ladders in order to rotate the stock so that the better-selling titles have prime real estate, right at eye level, and the less popular ones go higher up or lower down. Your books are bam in the middle. Mine are either very high or very low.

I often visit the Booksmith—sometimes to talk with Lisa,

sometimes, obviously, to buy books, occasionally to pick up a last-minute present (they maintain a pragmatically large gift section). One day, about two years ago, on my way to the pharmacy, I popped in to say a quick hello. When I found Lisa busy with a customer—a white, middle-aged woman in a camel hair coat—I perused the table with the sign over it that says "Books We Love." As I thumbed through one of the newer releases, I overheard Lisa telling the woman in the coat, "These books will change your life. In a good way," and turned to find her pressing the first three volumes of *My Struggle* into the woman's hands. The customer was clearly hesitant. Maybe she didn't want to spend so much money on three books at once, when of course there was no guarantee she'd like even the first one. Or maybe she didn't want to make such a huge time commitment. Books 1-3 alone, after all, clock in at nearly 1,500 pages. Then again, maybe she didn't quite trust Lisa. The thought did occur to me. Lisa has slightly wild green eyes. They glitter. "Just buy Book 1, then," she said. "When you're done you can come back and buy Book 2. It will be your reward."

Lisa's one of the best readers I know, so I was intrigued by her assertion that *My Struggle* could change a person's life in a *good* way. Which is why, a couple of minutes later, I found myself coughing up sixteen dollars and change for Book 1, despite my annoyance at the photo on its cover.

I began reading that very afternoon, and even now I distinctly remember two things from that early encounter. The first is this: I noticed an intense atmospheric shift on page 25, when, following three asterisks (which themselves follow an occasionally florid introductory passage about the physical characteristics of the heart and the fate of the human body after death), you begin writing about yourself sitting at your desk, crying perhaps (one eye is wet, the skin beneath it "dimly reflects a little light" in a window).

In this passage you inform the reader—with all the jollity of a man giving instructions to an engraver for his own headstone—of the precise date and time, your name, your birth year and month, your current age (thirty-nine), as well as the fact that you have three children and are on your second marriage. It goes on for a while in this vein, but what I remember most clearly is how those first few autobiographical sentences, so simple and factual, arrested me completely. It was as if my inner barometer had suddenly plummeted. If you had been speaking to me in person, I would have leaned in. But of course you weren't. The second thing I remember is how boring I found what followed—a couple hundred pages detailing a tedious teenage escapade of yours involving beer and a New Year's Eve party. It was the whole hiding-the-beer-in-the-snow thing that made me put down the book. I forgot about it for a while.

And yet something of those early pages stayed with me. So much so that when I had the opportunity to present on a panel at a writers' conference in Iceland in May of 2017, but was undecided about whether or not I should go (time, money, social anxiety), the fact that you were giving the keynote turned out to be a significant item in the "pro" column. Though really it was the draw of Iceland itself that convinced my husband and me to buy five tickets to Reykjavik. Everyone was going: James, both our kids, and—in a somewhat unexpected turn of events—my father.

Your father, of course, is a central figure in *My Struggle*: an intimidating man, tall, charismatic, and cruel, who projects onto you, his youngest child, relentless accusations of idiocy and effeminacy. According to your depiction, he seemed incapable of not tormenting you, even though, on some level, every instance of his small-scale sadism—chiseled and merciless and focused on minutiae as meaningless as a missing sock—seemed to cause him as much emotional anguish as it did you. It's the death of this fragile yet brutal man that forms the untouchable axis around which all six volumes of *My Struggle* orbit. As we learn over the course of Book 1, your father died of a heart attack that occurred while he was drunk and installed in an armchair in front of the television in his mother's living room, surrounded by empty vodka bottles scattered all over the floor. But, as you explain, there's also the possibility that he didn't actually die *in* the armchair, only near it. Yes, it could have been that your father's body fell out of the armchair at some point *before* the actual moment of death. Or it could have fallen out of the chair *after* his death. On this point, torturous as it is to you, you're never granted clarity. A fall, in any case, at one point or another, is the only thing that seems to make sense of the broken nose and crimson cheeks that disfigure your father's face so grotesquely in death, as you and your brother, Yngve, discover while viewing his corpse at the chapel. Only this much seems certain: the last time your father was seen by human eyes (your grandmother's), and at least assumed to be alive, he was sitting in that armchair.

My father, incidentally, is also an alcoholic. He has decades of recovery behind him at this point, but my memories of him during his worst years as a drunk also involve an armchair—upholstered in ochre-colored crushed velvet. When I was a teenager, he spent enormous stretches of time in this chair, staring intently at nothing, not moving a muscle. If you spoke to him, he wouldn't respond. He was feeling sorry for himself. I didn't know it back then, but I do now. At least I think I know it. But of course I don't. Because how can we really know anything about the inner life of a fellow human being?

They're back. I can hear them—James and Jonah—chatting as they walk down the concrete path to our door. Jonah's bouncing a soccer ball. James' voice is deep, just a low, indistinct mumble. I can't understand what he's saying, but his tone sounds instructive. I guess it's time to sign off. There's still dinner to make. Laundry to hang. Et cetera. I hope to pick this up again soon. But for now—and with heartiest congratulations on the birth of your youngest child—I am—

Cordially yours,
Kim Adrian

March 5, 2019

Dear Mr. Knausgaard,

Shortly after I returned home from the conference in Iceland that I mentioned in my last letter, I had lunch with Lisa at a little Japanese restaurant two blocks from the bookstore. She wanted to hear all about my trip.

"Was it amazing? Was it elemental? Was it brutally beautiful? So much so that you no longer feel ordinary life can sustain you in this lovely but inherently sterile suburban oasis we call Brookline?" Lisa often talks like this, like she's a book, even though she doesn't write, just reads a lot.

We were eating our favorite thing on the menu: veggie tempura. It's a good deal because not only do they give you a heaping stack of deep-fried veggies, as well as a bowl of miso soup, a mound of rice, and a small crunchy salad, but also several miniature piles of exotic pickles and musky-smelling beans (I think they're beans). It's good, not great—but it takes a long time to eat and that, really, is the point.

I told Lisa that Iceland had been all the things she'd said, especially elemental, and I shared a few highlights from that part of the trip when we drove up and down the west coast of the island: the eerie volcanic fields, the gleaming, zipper-like glaciers, the maddening wind, the yellow nights, the flossy waterfalls. I told her about how expensive the restaurants had been (a single slice of carrot cake = $15) and how, as a result, we'd cooked nearly all of our meals at the Airbnb's we'd rented. I praised the butter, the milk, the eggs, and the potatoes, all of which had been unusually rich and delicious, not to mention comparatively cheap, and which, as a result, we'd eaten in great quantities. Then I said, "And, oh, yeah, I heard Knausgaard speak. He gave the keynote at the conference."

Lisa happened to be taking a sip of water when I said this, and as the words came out of my mouth she started choking. Her face went bright red as she coughed and spluttered. The waiter came out of the kitchen to see what was going on. He stood a few feet behind her, looking concerned, but said nothing because the wait staff at that restaurant is seriously class-A, despite the mediocrity of the food they're forced to serve. I patted her on the back and asked if she was okay.

"Yes," she said hoarsely. Her eyes were watering. "I'm fine. But you can't just say things like that. You can't just lay that on me."

She then explained how intense it had been for her to read *My Struggle*—Books 1-5 of it in any case (Book 6 had not yet been published in English). She'd read those books in a kind of frenzy, she said, every minute she wasn't working. Her husband found this so irritating he actually suggested she not come home until she was finished, so she'd gotten a room at the local Sheraton Inn and read straight through the weekend. "It was blissful," she said. "One of the best gifts he's ever given me."

I wonder if this was how the woman in Iceland read your work. There were many women in Iceland, obviously, but only two who've stayed in my mind. One gave me excellent knitting advice, the other was the woman who sat next to me during your keynote at the Harpa Centre in Reykjavik. Your speech was open to the public that night, not just to us conference goers, and the difference between the two populations was obvious. The conference goers—writers, largely American, some Australian—were dressed more or less as both my daughter and I were that evening, which is to say in sporty, serviceable travel duds. But the Icelanders who'd come to hear you speak were for the most part more formally attired. The woman who sat next to me, for instance, wore a remarkable outfit consisting of dozens of elegant strips of gray fabric, roughly cut and artfully assembled. The effect was kind of bohemian fairy-witch. She was perhaps in her early sixties, slender, silver-haired, probably pretty when she was younger, but you couldn't call her that now. There was something decidedly hungry about her face, I noticed, when she gave both my daughter, Nina, and me an obvious sizing up as she sidled past us to take her seat, just to the right of me in the fourth row.

You were introduced at some length by, if I remember correctly, the Norwegian ambassador to Iceland, who called you by your full name, which sounded so great—the "Karl" smashing into the "Ove," and the "Knausgaard" nothing at all the way I say it, with my American accent, but a weird mash-up of angular and singsong sounds. You then hulked up to the podium, all six-foot whatever of you, and without the usual niceties (the ambassador got no thanks; the conference staff none; the audience nada) you simply began reading from *Autumn*, your latest book in English translation, and the first one you wrote after having finished *My Struggle*. Virtually as soon as you'd opened your mouth, the entire auditorium—which was enormous and packed to the gills, and which had only seconds earlier been buzzing with palpable anticipation—went perfectly still. It was as if everyone were holding their breath. Was this on account of what you were reading? Or was it because of the way you read it? I still can't decide. I do like the opening pages of *Autumn*, those in which you address your fourth child, an as-yet unborn daughter, but are they really so jaw-dropping as that? I was surprised by the hush. Still, your delivery was intense. Dramatic without being overtly theatrical. Soft, almost gentle, yet at the same time there was the feeling that something important hung in the balance, when it came to your words. You gripped the sides of the podium with both hands. Your gray hair hung over your brow. You said, "The world expresses its being, but we are not listening, and since we are no longer immersed in it, experiencing it as a part of ourselves, it is as if it escapes us." And everyone was still. Everyone, that is, but the woman sitting next to me, who started doing this weird thing, pressing her left thigh against my right thigh. I couldn't tell at first if this was a sexual gesture, or maybe a passive-aggressive one, or perhaps completely unintentional. Though after a while the pressure grew, so I figured she had to know what she was doing. I moved my leg, but she soon found it again and pressed some more. Eventually I had to angle myself entirely away from her and toward Nina, who sat to my left, but before I did so I glanced at the woman's face to find that she was staring up at you with an almost beatific expression on her worn features. It frankly freaked me out. What was it, exactly, that she heard as you spoke? Was it really so different from what I heard? Or was she transfixed by something else, something beyond or beside the words themselves? Your physical person, perhaps? The soothing, almost lullaby cadence of your voice? Or something else—something more private and convoluted. Because you are a bit of a symbol, I've noticed, to a lot of people. Though of exactly what, I'm not sure.

Kim Adrian

March 11, 2019

Dear Knausgaard,

It was starting to feel a little coy, my calling you "Mr. Knausgaard." But it's a tricky question. What should I call you? I've settled, for the moment, on "Knausgaard," since that's how I refer to you in conversation. Though to tell the truth I'm not a hundred percent sure what I actually mean when I say "you" in these missives. I only know that when I think of "you," that person is not entirely Knausgaard, the celebrated writer, nor entirely Karl Ove, the protagonist of your most famous work, but a kind of hybrid creature: part Knausgaard, part Karl Ove, part me. Because how I perceive you depends entirely on how *I* perceive you. Meaning, I am necessarily part of that equation. This is just as true in real life, with real people, I suppose, but the shadow cast by one's own self over the perception of others is harder to discern in life than it is in books. Maybe there's just not enough time, in the unceasing flow of daily living, to parse things so carefully. But books you can put down and pick up. And you can think about them in between.

> "The essential difference between a book and
> a friend is not their greater or lesser wisdom, but
> the manner in which we communicate with them,
> reading being the exact opposite of conversation."
> —Marcel Proust

"KOK" is actually what I call you in the privacy of my own mind. And KOK (pronounced "coke," in my head) is someone or something I'm actually quite familiar with, though if I could paint a picture of the KOK I know, I doubt you, yourself, would recognize him. That said, we have a pretty good relationship—KOK and I. Which isn't to say he's not a pain in the ass sometimes. There have been months at a stretch when I've had to stop dealing with him entirely just to get a little oxygen back in my life, or to get over some unwittingly nasty misogynist gibe he's made. KOK is how I refer to you/not-you in all my marginalia, scrawled, in greater or lesser quantities, in .5mm mechanical pencil, on the pages of *My Struggle*. There's quite a bit of it, at least in Books 1-3, Book 5, and Book 6. (Book 4, sorry—I could barely get through it; its margins are bare.)

Ciao for now,
KA

P.S. It's fun pretending I'm writing you letters. But obviously these are not really letters—not entirely, not exclusively. They are also parts of a book. And recently I find myself worrying that you, Knausgaard, might someday find occasion to read this book, and that possibility is beginning to make me nervous. I worry, for instance, that you might not be as pristinely ego-less as KOK, who always listens to my opinions without batting an eyelash. Hell, he doesn't even have eyelashes. For the most part, I try to put thoughts of you, the person, Karl Ove Knausgaard, out of my head because, technically speaking, this is strictly between KOK and myself, and KOK already knows perfectly well what I think about *My Struggle*. For instance, he knows that I found Book 6 exhausting, and not in a good way. I know what it's like to be exhausted by a book in a good way. But Book 6 exhausted me in a way that felt arbitrary. Capricious. Stubborn. No—dogmatic. That's the word I'm looking for. But I'm getting ahead of myself.

March 16, 2019

Dear Knausgaard,

James once read an excerpt from your soccer book, *Home and Away: Writing the Beautiful Game*, in one of his magazines, but he didn't enjoy it. He said it was self-indulgent. He says *My Struggle* sounds self-indulgent, too, when he listens to me talk about it. He even has a theory about my obsession with your "self-indulgent" work. He says I have an unnatural level of patience for self-indulgent people, on account of my upbringing. That's how he put it, but he meant my father. James thinks my father is why I'm not only able to stomach your work, but also why I find it so infinitely fascinating. He senses Freudian tangles. It's possible. And I sense, at times, in him, a complicated, twice-referred Oedipal impatience. The other day, for instance, he interrupted my explanation of—something (I forget—maybe your treatment of shame in *My Struggle*?)—to say, "You know, you never really told me what it's actually about. The whole thing."

"It's just his life."

"But what's the story?"

"It's just the story of him writing it."

"Really?"

"Well, according to him, it's about 'recapturing the world.'

He says he wants to make the world 'real' again."

"But the world *is* real," said James.

... continued
(after staring at a bowl of speckled pears)

You've got to admit, he has a point.

... (after two cups of tea and a hazelnut cookie)

Many things happen in My Struggle, of course. You bury your father, fall in love, have children, write a novel, get depressed, write another novel, a really huge one. But what *is* the story?

I don't know. Maybe I was right when I said the story is about you writing it. Because literature, in your view, is of a higher value than nearly anything else. All your deepest aspirations are bound up in it. In Book 2, you describe your aims this way:

> I had to cut all my ties with the flattening, thoroughly corrupt world of culture where everyone, every single little upstart, was for sale, cut all my ties with the vacuous TV and newspaper world, sit down in a room and read in earnest, not contemporary literature but literature of the highest quality, and then write as if my life depended on it.

My Struggle may not tell a story in any conventional sense of the word, but it certainly is a struggle, and every struggle is a kind of story, and every story involves a struggle, so maybe you're covered.

But if I had to describe the novel as a whole to someone like my husband (which I don't; he lost interest), I'd say that each of its six books concerns a different time period of your life. Though that makes it sound like an autobiography, and it's not that at all, because an autobiography, no matter how artful, is a fairly straightforward construction focused on the domino chains of cause and effect that shape a person's life. And this is not your intention in *My Struggle*. No, your intention is much simpler—so simple it sounds ridiculous, it sounds like nothing: you merely want to write about life as you experience it.

And yet reading *My Struggle* isn't like reading a teenager's self-obsessed diary. It's no navel-gazing exercise. For one thing—despite all the digressions—you're actually very careful to keep your reader's needs in mind on many counts, including the narrative one, in the sense that each of the books that comprise the novel as a whole does have some kind of an arc, no matter how loosely slung. And these smaller shapes provide just enough narrative tug to keep a reader on track for the long haul.

Book 1, for instance, is shaped primarily by your father's death and its disorienting aftermath, which involves a lot of cleaning at your grandmother's house, in Kristiansand, where your father had been living. The place is a wreck, and all this cleaning has deep metaphorical implications, though for me these sank in only slowly, because the writing itself never gives off that telltale whiff (slightly metallic?) of a well-constructed metaphor, but instead evokes only—and much more straightforwardly—the smells of bleach, cleansing powder, soap, and ammonia. So even though there's no plot to speak of, you do work your way into something, and then—almost—past it: the pain of being your father's son.

... (another cup of tea)

One of the things I like best about *My Struggle* is how hodgepodge it is—narrative, essay, and philosophical excursions occur in no particular order, combination, or ratio. This mash-up is especially apparent in Book 2, with its loose, unhurried spirals of reflection, through which you weave a detailed account of falling in love with Linda Böstrom, your second wife, as well as the sweet and sour ordeal of moving in together, having children, and generally sharing a life. The tang of suspense that haunts this volume has to do, I think, with the slow-motion way in which your relationship starts to go off the rails almost as soon as it begins: Linda's manic depression and your manic ambition are simply not a good combination. But the adagio drama of a failing marriage isn't what kept me going in Book 2. No, what kept me going was all the hodge-podge. This could be described as the motion of your mind, and certainly that's part of it. A mind is always interesting. But I think what's really captivating is how the hodge-podge character of it all functions as a kind of demonstration, a demonstration of freedom—freedom in the way you approach the task at hand, which, in this case, of course, is the writing of a novel, a novel whose very substance is a hundred percent at odds with the more or less homogenous texture found so often in contemporary novels steeped, for instance, in the conventions of realism, where tonal consistency is deemed a necessary component of what John Gardener famously described as the earmark of all great literature: the maintenance of a "vivid and continuous dream." You have zero desire to deposit the reader in such a perfectly constructed dreamworld. You want to do just the opposite. But then there's Book 3.

I've heard you, in interviews, cringe about the quality of the writing in this book because in it you adopt the diction and outlook of a child, just as you match the pitch of your voice to the age you were when the main events in each book took place. In Book 3, which treats your childhood years, this is an especially risky operation, thus your public worries that your voice in it sounds "idiotic." Though to be honest, I can never tell, with you, what counts for real modesty, real chagrin, and what might be, instead, brilliantly camouflaged false versions of these things. Because that book is genius. Well, at least I loved it. In fact, I rushed to read it whenever I could, which I can't say of the others. It reminded me of a snow globe. Meaning, in its pages there was a whole world full of the tiniest and most impossible details. And there was a lot of snow.

The motley aspect of things extends, too, to the quality of the books themselves in the sense that some are better than others. And one is very bad. This is strictly IMHO, obviously, but Book 4 is a real stinker. I couldn't stand it—your attempt at the artist-as-a-young-man thing. You must have been unbearable at eighteen. At least, the young man you project through your eighteen-year-old voice is exactly the kind of young man I couldn't abide when I was that age, and the kind I've never been able to stomach since, in classrooms, when teaching, for instance. Constantly horny, often inebriated, wildly self-infatuated. Maybe it's just proof that you did exactly what you set out to do—capture the personality and outlook of your eighteen-year-old self— but I had no patience. More than that, the whole thing felt fake to me. Constructed. Thinly realist in all the most boring, mechanistic ways. As if it were chugging away at something. Setting the stage, perhaps, for Book 5—which, it's true, might not have made as much sense without the biographical facts you set out in Book 4, in which you get a teaching job in northern Norway, get drunk all the time, develop a disabling crush on a thirteen-year-old student, figure out how to masturbate (took you a while), call home every so often, reconcile yourself to your parents' divorce, and try your hand at writing short stories. I missed the delicacy and magic of Book 3, and couldn't wait to be done with the fourth. If skimming didn't run counter to my nature, I would have skimmed, but unfortunately it does.

... (three olives and a sliver of halvah)

Book 5 begins just the next year, but there's far more vitality in the voice department for some reason. There's still a lot of masturbation, a lot of drinking, and more writing, as you've been admitted to a prestigious literary arts program at the University of Bergen. In this volume we get to know your brother, Yngve, a little better, and he's a real tonic. I was always happy to see Yngve's name on the page, mostly because you were (almost) always happy to see him. The affection the two of you have for each other is one of the sweetest elements of *My Struggle*—almost as sweet as the sticky, soft, intermittent presence of your children. Reading about Yngve often reminded me of my sister, because she's a lot like him—sensible, steady, supportive, smart (but never needing to prove it). Your tone shifts a lot in this volume as you grow into adulthood, study art history, and fall madly in love a few times. Though still prone to drinking binges and high drama in the romance department, intellectually you're getting more complicated, and as the book advances, it increasingly concerns your thoughts about and investigations into the nature of art and literature. I was once again a happy camper.

The timeframe of Book 6 is far more recent than the others, opening, as it does, on the eve of the publication of Book 1, after which it traces the conception, composition, publication, and problematic aftermath (both public and personal) of all the other books, as well as the unfolding process of writing the book in the reader's hands. In other words, we're in serious meta-territory with this one. It's also in Book 6 that you plunk your 400-page essay about Hitler, "The Name and the Number," which is a complete departure from the rest of the novel—more formal, almost academic in tone, and more purely philosophical in intent.

A four-hundred page essay on Hitler! That's crazy, man.

—*Kim A.*

March 21, 2019

Dear Knausgaard,

In Iceland—do you remember?—somebody asked why you call *My Struggle* a novel, not a memoir or an autobiography, since it concerns your own experience of your own life. You answered that *My Struggle* is a "nonfiction novel," then clarified by explaining that the content of all six books belongs to the realm of nonfiction (which is to say, "real life"), but the way in which you chose to treat that content was novelistic. To justify this adjective—*novelistic*—you focused on the element of time, the flow of which, you said, you'd worked to dilate and constrict according to conventions we more readily associate with the novel than with memoir or, certainly, autobiography. At the time I remember thinking this seemed a rather limited view of memoir, but I also understood what you were getting at. Now, however, I wonder if your answer may have been a little disingenuous. Perhaps you were tired? (Another question—the first of the evening—concerned your impressions of Iceland: Did you like it? You answered somewhat testily that you'd only just gotten off the plane a couple of hours earlier.)

Since that night, nearly two years ago now, I've spent quite a bit of time with *My Struggle*, and have considered this question of fiction/nonfiction/novel/memoir from several angles. By this point, I'm convinced that the work is as full of fiction as it is of nonfiction. Not that it matters. Well, yes it does. But it also doesn't. I mean, it's a big question: What is fiction? What is "real life"? How different are they, really? Can we actually separate them in any kind of meaningful way? At any rate, the distinction seemed to matter a great deal to the person who asked you that question in Reykjavik. And what you neglected to say at the time, which I wish you had, is that there is in truth a tremendous amount of invention in the pages of *My Struggle*. For instance, if I grab the volume closest to me—Book 3—and open it at random, there is on page 63 a scene that finds you sitting on a stool in the kitchen of your childhood home, chatting with your mother as she makes dinner. You are just beginning school, which puts you around the age of five:

"I wish we had a cat I could play with," I said. "Can't we have a cat?"

"That would be nice," Mom said. "I like cats.

They're good company."

"So is it Dad who doesn't like them then?"

"I don't know," Mom said. "He's just not that interested, I think. And he probably thinks they're a bit too much work."

"But I can take care of it," I said. "That's no problem."

"I know," Mom said. "We'll have to wait and see."

"Wait and see, wait and see," I said. "But if

Yngve wants a cat, that'll make three of us." Mom laughed.

"It's not that simple," she said. "You'll have to be

patient. Who knows what will happen."

She put the peeled carrot on the board and chopped it up, lifted the board, and slid the pieces into the large pot where there were already bones and bits of meat. I looked out of the window. Through the many small holes in the orange curtain Mom had crocheted I could see the road outside was empty, which it invariably was in the middle of the day.

It goes on from here, of course—the flow of scene and dialogue is nearly constant in Book 3. As I've said, I found this book mesmerizing. So much so that I hardly allowed the obvious question to enter my thoughts: *How does he remember such tiny details?* A single peeled carrot, chopped up and slid into the pot... Bones and bits of meat. A verbal exchange between mother and son without the least iota of doubt injected into its flow. I frankly didn't care how you'd managed it, I was happy simply to be under the book's unhurried spell. And yet it seems obvious that the dense thatch of details that crowd this and all the other volumes of *My Struggle* would require one of two things: a photographic memory or invention. You have often insisted, both in the work itself and in interviews, that you have a lousy memory, so why, then, in Iceland, didn't you admit that this "nonfiction novel" is also fictional in the sense that you'd invented thousands upon thousands of details, no matter how apt or likely or—taken singly—inconsequential they may be? Were you resistant to muddy the waters that divide fact and fiction since the whole premise of *My Struggle* rests on the idea that the work is based on your own life—or, rather, your experience of your own life, your own *real* life? Did you worry, that night, that admitting to any degree of invention might, in some readers' eyes, undermine that premise? Or were you instead reluctant to parse the limiting terms of the man's question because you are interested in only one thing: literature, pure literature, literature of the freest and most radical kind, which, like life itself, takes zero heed of such categories? Or were you just tired?

In an interview in the *New Yorker* that Lisa emailed me a link to months ago and that I have not yet read because I cannot seem to get past the slo-mo black and white animated GIF of your glowering face lifting dramatically, even a little threateningly toward the viewer—those deep-set eyes, that hawklike nose, your carefully-carelessly feathered hair and unsmiling mouth all eerily suggestive of a massive bird of prey—you say (I know only because the quote is highlighted at the top of the article, next to the GIF), "The duty of literature is to fight fiction. It's to find a way into the world as it is." Leaving aside the flaccid irony of its juxtaposition with the glamorous GIF, this quote does a lot to explain your insistence, in *My Struggle*, on a patient examination of the smallest details of everyday life. It explains, as well, the insertion of the 400-plus page Hitler essay in Book 6, and the necessary exercise of compare/contrast you implicitly ask every serious reader of *My Struggle* to engage in due to its title, which of course gestures boldly toward the massive autobiographical tome Hitler wrote by the same name, only in German. This obviously is a question I have asked myself many times: In what way does your *Min Kamp* differ from Hitler's *Mein Kampf*? Does your struggle, as some reviewers have suggested, concern the challenges of changing diapers and making dinner while still maintaining a life of the mind? Yes, in a sense, but really it's much broader than that. As you indicate in the GIF-quote, your struggle is a search for the *real*. But what is that?

> "Beyond the fiction of reality, there is the reality of fiction."
> —Slavoj Žižek

Hitler's *Mein Kampf*, according to your analysis, is replete with fiction, or, to put it another way, ideology. In its pages, Hitler paints a picture of himself as an ambitious young man who twists and strives toward an ideal, a utopian vision, a seductive fantasy, a highly romanticized vision of his "homeland," and this vision eventually comes to infect his fellow citizens, because, yes, fiction is infectious. Over time, through the influence of this fiction-infection, those citizens would act in ways that not only destroyed millions upon millions of lives but also changed humanity forever. In Hitler's *My Struggle*, you explain, "a single human life is of little value." But in *your* struggle it's the other way around. *Min Kamp* strives to illuminate the countless gross and subtle movements of that operation we call life as it surges through just a single biological entity.

Put another way, Hitler's struggle was directed toward society as a whole and it was expressed through rhetoric, or the art of persuasive speech delivered to huge crowds. But *your* struggle is conducted on the grounds of literature and seeks neither to persuade nor manipulate, but only to express and reveal, often by a process of sly destruction (exposing corrosive fictions within a fictional context). On top of that, as a work of literature, *Min Kamp* is directed not toward society as a whole—that nameless mass—but toward what you at one point call the "unfamiliar reader." Which is to say another single biological entity. Unspecified yet discrete. Hi.

—*Kim*

March 24, 2019

Dear Knausgaard,

I was tempted, at first, to call my husband "David" in these letters, but that's not his name. His name is James. My daughter's name is Nina, although I almost called her "Isabella." And Jonah I almost called "Isaac." It just felt so strange to type out their real names. Like lifting a curtain. But also like rough handling.

I got into the habit of using these false names while writing a memoir that had mostly to do with my relationship to my mother. The false name I gave her was Linda. The name I gave my father was Jake. My sister became Tracy. I usually say that the reason I gave everyone in that book a false name was in order to protect their privacy because the memoir deals not only with my mother's mental illness, but with incest, drug and alcohol addiction, domestic abuse, and a stabbing. But to be honest, I did it at least as much for my own sake. Because the only way I could write about these things—or, rather, about my own memories and perceptions of these things—was to put a kind of shield between myself and the people I was afraid of hurting.

You, of course, do just the opposite in *My Struggle*, insisting on using real names whenever possible. In Book 6 you write: "The name is what joins the body to our social life, the name collects all judgments and assumptions as to a particular personality, and what happens when a person dies is that the name is no longer connected to the body, which decomposes and disappears, whereas the name lives on in the social world." In other words, the name functions as a kind of interface between the individual and society. This is also more or less how you view the emotion of shame—as a kind of fence stretched between these same two entities, a firm but not infallible boundary made of pain and humiliation that lets us know exactly what we should keep inside and what we can afford to let out, into the social realm.

Shame in many ways indicates the precise juncture between the inner life of the individual and the outer expression of that life, which is the very juncture that *My Struggle* works so hard to explore. I'd even go so far as to say that your insistence on openness—or, to put it another way, personal freedom—is actually an experimental confrontation with the emotion of shame conducted on the grounds of literature.

It's a clever arrangement. Brilliant, really. Because the act of writing itself, like names and like the emotion of shame, is also a hybrid thing: both public and private. Public in the sense that it's essentially a social act (as all linguistic acts are at root social); private in the sense that it's done in isolation. And because shame doesn't enter into the equation when we're alone—because, as you point out, we can have the most radical or antisocial or disgusting or simply idiotic thoughts then, and not be ashamed of them since they exist only inside of us—it's much easier (though not exactly easy) when writing to circumvent the knee-jerk reactions and repressions that shame has instilled in us over the course of our lifetimes. In short, you use writing very strategically as a way of bypassing shame, letting everything from the inside flow onto the page and quite consciously refusing to let it filter through the membrane of shame.

Where you get into trouble, of course, is with other people—not only in saying exactly what you think about them, how you perceive them, remember them, and interact with them, but in using their real names on top of that. Because you really let it rip. Anyone who crosses your path is fair game—from your wife to your kids to the lady ringing you up at the grocery store. You put it all on the page: their foibles, their confessions, their reckless self-expression. This does more damage to some than to others. Linda fares especially badly. And your father's side of the family is furious with your depictions of your father and grandmother (the drinking, the incontinence, the filth), which I can understand, but it's also sad, ironic really, as that section, in Book 1, contains some of the most beautiful writing in the entire novel. And by beautiful I suppose mean generous. Because even though you always stay very much inside your own head, the portrait you draw of your grandmother, in particular, is one of incredible compassion. To her, for some reason, you allot more empathy than to anyone else in the novel outside of your children.

I guess, in the end, it's just a rude thing to do: using people's real names. But it's strange that such a simple, straightforward act should be so offensive. That both social and literary conventions should dictate so rigidly the use of false names in a setting like a novel, and that to buck those conventions should cause such a stir. Then again, maybe it's not so strange. Because using a person's real name is a kind of exposure, a transgression, even a kind of intrusion or incursion into the very realm you're so obsessed with: the private sphere. Only, instead of exposing that sphere from the inside, for yourself, you attack it from the outside, effectively ripping away the boundary between the inner and the outer, exposing the intimate secrets of others, and in this way subjecting them to the very emotion you, yourself, strive so desperately to escape. I'm talking about shame, of course.

Yet despite it all—your use of real names, your ruthless honesty—*My Struggle* doesn't quite avoid the cakey whiff of fiction, the 2-D vibe, the flat light of simulacra. Granted, it's hard to see most of the time. But it's there. For instance, take Tonje.

As a whole, *My Struggle* provides a nearly complete account of your life, with one notable exception—those years, in your late twenties and early thirties, when you were married to your first wife, Tonje. What a strange omission. A whole marriage. Yet it never bothered me as a reader. I didn't particularly feel the need to know about those years. I had plenty to chew on as it was. But as a person, I admit I'm curious. Not so much about the omission as about Tonje. How did she, alone, evade your efforts to make the world "real" again? What's odd is, despite the fact that she's barely in it, Tonje is in a way the most real-seeming person in the novel. Perhaps because she exists mostly outside of it.

—K. Adrian

April 16, 2019

Dear Knausgaard,

> *Boredom is the dream bird that*
> *hatches the egg of experience.*

I've read Walter Benjamin's essay "The Storyteller" several times over the last decade or so, and every time I bump into that line—which is how Benjamin describes the relationship of boredom to stories—it stops me in my tracks. What is a dream bird? What is an egg of experience? How can boredom hatch one?

As is the case with so many of Benjamin's more eccentric assertions, this one seems to mean many things at once. I bring it up now because one of those things applies to *My Struggle*, in the sense that there are hundreds of pages in your novel—maybe even the majority of pages—in which the prose can accurately be described as boring in precisely this way: a procreative way. I mean, plodding as it is, something comes alive.

For example:

Dad put two chops, three potatoes, and a small pile of fried onions on my plate. Sat down and heaped his plate.

"Well?" he said. "Anything new at school?" I shook my head.

"You didn't learn anything today?"

"No."

"No, of course not." We ate in silence.

Or this:

I picked John up and carried him to the bathroom after the others. I put him down on the floor, got the detergent from on top of the cupboard and sprinkled the white Ajax powder into the bottom of the bath, got the scouring pad from under the sink, moistened it, and began scrubbing the enamel. As it dissolved in the water, the white powder not only became liquid, it turned yellow too. I was fond of yellow. Yellow on white, yellow on green, yellow on blue. I liked lemons, their shape as well as their color...

Or:

I sat down and kept eating. After a while I picked up the tea pot and poured. Dark brown, almost like wood, the tea rose inside the white cup. A few leaves swirled and floated up, the others lay like a black mat at the bottom. I added milk, three teaspoons of sugar, stirred, waited until the leaves had settled on the bottom, and drank.

Mmm.

I've often wondered how you swing it—this near total rejection of craft, of style. It shouldn't work, but it does, I think because in rejecting both of these things you foreground what's left: your voice. And *that* works because your voice is such a good one—somber with occasional hints of mild humor, often clumsy or flatfooted, but at the same time, every once in a spine-tingling while, vaguely Biblical in tone. Most of all, it's a voice fed by a rich unrelenting wellspring of complex thought, memory, and emotion. It also works, I think, because you've actually considered quite carefully one aspect of craft—the most important one of all: the whole form/content relationship. Because despite surface appearances (and the disdainful laments of many critics), you've managed to marry these elements almost seamlessly in the sense that it's only your raw, unadorned voice that can convey (hold, carry, form) the true subject of *My Struggle* with any integrity at all. That subject, your quest—to make the world "real" again—is achievable (according to you) only through the act of revealing the innermost life of a single human being, not because that inner life—yours—is so special, but because, practically speaking, it's the only one you have access to, and because it's only there, on the inside, that reality unfolds in its least distorted form.

... continued (4:15 pm)

The bouquet of flowers James bought me last week—carnations, calla lilies, and stock—has wilted. The stems of the flowers have begun to soften and rot. It smells bad, but at the same time there's an intriguing cinnamon note swirling around in the funk.

Rotting flowers always remind me of Kenzaburo Oë's

A Personal Matter because he talks about them a lot in that book—the way the stench of dozens of decomposing plants filled his home in the weeks after his brain-damaged son was born. I've only experienced Oë's work in translation (just as I've only experienced your books in translation), but I remember reading something Oë's primary translator, John Nathan, once said about how Oë's writing, in Japanese, is super clunky and awkward, perhaps even more clunky and awkward than it is in English. In fact, Japanese readers often complain that it sounds almost as if it's been translated—rather badly—*out* of English. Which means actually translating it *into* English is an especially tricky operation. Nathan also mentions in this same essay that Oë's natural style is quite fluid, really very graceful, but that after the first draft, he works hard to clog things up, syntactically speaking, and to make strange his word choices because he believes in the usefulness of what the Russian Formalists called "defamiliarization," a concept I know you mention at least once or twice in *My Struggle*, but god knows where. Finding quotes in that thing is a nightmare.

Despite the fact that your work is, aesthetically speaking, almost the polar opposite of Oë's, you still manage to achieve the same thing, the same kind of defamiliarization. But instead of making your word choice unexpected or your syntax weird, and in this way forcing the reader to slow down and pay closer attention to the text so that they can really *see* what's being described, you speed everything up so the sentences feel very smooth, simple, natural. There's almost no resistance at all. Your diction, at least in the more narrative passages, tends toward the ordinary, the conversational, even the naive (that "Mmm" with the tea, for instance). And yet you still manage to make the world seem vivid and—yes—a little more real. For instance, this scene, in Book 6, which finds you examining the kitchen in your Malmö apartment early one morning:

> Outside, the sun was coming up over the horizon. Its rays were sharp and penetrated the room. Everything became visible in its light, the bits of food on the floor, the trail of coffee stains that ran from the counter on the right to the sink on the other side, the globules of fat that specked the surface of the sausage water in the saucepan, the two bloated sausages that lay at the bottom, split open, the two empty milk cartons next to it, the open packet of margarine, so soft it was almost a fluid, its yellow color much deeper now than when it had been taken from the fridge. The Wetex cloth, stiff as a shell when dry, draped over the lip of metal that separated the twin bowls of the sink, like some odd fitting that was a part of it, originally white, now a grimy gray.

The passage continues from there, running four or even five times as long as what I've quoted. It should be dead boring. The words and the way you put them together are so normal. Not quite conversational, but so very ordinary. Almost like thought, but articulated. Strangely, the unremittingness of it all, the way your gaze moves so patiently around the room as you describe everything it encounters—a transparent cheese wrapper, a chopping board with beet juice stains, a line of withered, potted plants, a jug of water with tiny bubbles in it—creates a feeling of suspense (or some close cousin of suspense). In most fiction, a description of this kind would serve its purpose after only a line or two: the sunlight, the withered plants, the pan with the grease-specked water would be plenty. Because in most fiction the point would be to set a scene. But you don't write scenes. You write perceptions of reality. And for some reason that's totally intoxicating.

My Struggle has been consistently hailed as radical, even revolutionary in its immediacy, its honesty, and its confessional disclosures. Yet of course these are nothing new in the realm of the novel. Oë and his compatriots in Japan, for instance, have been honing these aspects of first-person narration in the so-called "I-novel" and its descendants for over a century. Jack Kerouac and his fellow Beats worked to bypass the elegant white lies of stylistic refinement by writing "spontaneously" or "automatically," which is pretty much what you did, cranking out ten pages a day, five days a week, for four years straight, and hardly ever revising. Charles Bukowski detonated personal boundaries and exploited almost every relationship in his life for the sake of his obsessive fiction. On top of all this, confessional literature is as old as the hills (or, at least, as old as St. Augustine). So what's the deal? Why is *My Struggle* such a huge phenomenon? Maybe it's the Scandinavian flavor of your work that makes it seem so singular? Or maybe it's the quality of your game, because you *are* really good at it—the contrivance of all those anti-contrivances, your moody, Norwegian sprezzatura. Or maybe it's simply the novelty of a man writing about the domestic in such great detail—the tedious everyday trials and tribulations of raising young children, changing diapers, daycare drop-offs, ice cream bribes, grocery shopping, table setting, tub cleaning... But mostly I think *My Struggle* found the fame it has because, like every work of art that explodes on the scene, it's managed to hit a nerve, to make contact with some frictional element already chafing the atmosphere. In the case of *My Struggle* that element is the very thing that drove you to write the novel in the first place, which is to say the uneasy feeling that the world has become unreal, or, as you put it in Book 1, "the feeling that the world was small and that I grasped everything in it." This is the primary lament of *My Struggle*—the thing it fights against with every description of every cornflake, every diaper, every crayfish, every cigarette butt, every sunset, every sponge, every cup of tea...

> My basic feeling is that of the world disappearing, that our lives are being filled with images of the world, and that these images are inserting themselves between us and the world, making the world around us lighter and lighter and less and less binding. We are trying to detach ourselves from everything that ties us to physical reality; from the bloodless, vacuum-packed steaks in the refrigerated counters of our supermarkets, the industrially produced meat of cooped-up animals, to society's concealment of physical death and illness, from the cosmetically rectified uniformity of female faces to the endless flow of news images that pass through us every day and which together, in sum, erase all differences and establish a kind of universal sameness...

Yes, you definitely hit a nerve. Because don't we all have this sense? The feeling that the attenuation of something—our interactions with reality—has reached a truly dangerous point, has become so extreme that it's actually on the verge of snapping? Or has it already broken? Something, in any case, seems to have changed. Nothing sticks to anything anymore. You only have to click your mouse, and voilà. We've done something. Gone somewhere. And it's really weird here, where we're all so hungry all the time. We enter formulations to assuage this hunger in Google's search bar god knows how many times a day, punch the buttons on our remote controls, stare hopefully into our heavy little handheld rectangles of distraction hour after hour, but nothing fills us up. Nothing *can* fill us up but the very thing we turn away from, which is exactly what *My Struggle* reminds us to embrace: the world itself and our bodies in it—our bodies which, despite our best efforts, still pulse with life.

Off to check my Instagram account,
just kidding,
not really,
Kim

April 29, 2019

Dear Knausgaard,

I just spent the last thirty minutes watching YouTube videos of kids reacting to strange foods (natto, escargot, stargazy pie). There's a word for that in Sanskrit: *prajnaparadha*. "Crimes against wisdom."

It's Monday. Mondays are often hard for me to focus. I fall off the horse over the weekend and it takes all day for me to climb back on. This past weekend I sat at my desk just once and that was to print out something for my father, who was in town for the day. I made him a special dinner: pasta with shrimp cooked in cream. He kept me company while I was at the stove, offering bits of unsolicited advice (more salt in the water, less cream in the sauce). It made me nervous, and the dish didn't come out as good as it usually does. On Sunday, Jonah had the flu and needed many little ministrations while Nina, who's in college, had a minor crisis that had to be dealt with long distance. So I didn't write all weekend, which is usually the case, but I did manage to read a book. *The Fifth Child*, by Doris Lessing. It was okay. I didn't love it.

Have you by any chance read Javier Cercas' book *The Blind Spot: An Essay on the Novel*? It came out in English translation last year. I had it on pre-order weeks before its release on the basis of the title alone, and devoured it upon its arrival. It is a smart and graceful little book, the thesis of which argues that certain kinds of novels (those belonging to just one of the two strands that constitute, according to Milan Kundera, the bifurcated literary tradition we call "the novel") can be characterized as having at their center, always, a "blind spot." That's to say, a question, something unknown, a kind of void through which the novel pours itself, illuminating every aspect of that question, that unknown thing, without ever answering it. Blind spot novels, in other words, operate less by way of plot than paradox: the questions these kinds of novels pose remain unanswered precisely because they are unanswerable. Or, as Cercas puts it, "The answer is the very quest for an answer, the question itself, the book itself. The answer is a blind spot."

I liked *The Blind Spot* very much—and yet I also hated it. Why? Because I'm a woman. And because Cercas, although clearly an admirable thinker, is also a bit of a shit. Why? Because of the dozens of novels he investigates to support his elegant thesis, there is not a single novel by a woman. Why?

Of course, in the grand scheme of things, novels by women are still a relatively recent development. This is true as well of novels by people "of color," which is to say people of non-European origin, or with some element of non-European ancestry, as the tradition of the novel has since its inception (which Cercas locates in *Don Quixote*) been advanced largely by men, in particular white European men. Which isn't to say exclusively. Many, many women, and many, many people of non-European ancestry have written astonishing novels of exactly the kind Cercas celebrates, yet in his discussion he analyses only the novels of Herman Melville, Thomas Mann, Javier Marias, Jean-Paul Sartre, J.M. Coetzee, Franz Kafka, Mario Vargas Llosa, Italo Calvino, Truman Capote... On and on goes the list: Joseph Conrad, Umberto Eco, Michel Houellebecq, Georges Perec, Ernesto Sabato, you yourself, Gustave Flaubert, Giuseppe Tomasi di Lampedusa, Hunter S. Thompson, Jorge Luis Borges, Julian Barnes... All male writers. But why? Why *exclusively* male writers? Don't you find it a bit strange?

Even you, who have reasonably been accused of sexism in your reading habits, appreciate more female writers than zero. Even you, who—it must be said—celebrate the male lineage of the novel as a way of life if not an actual religion have at least dipped a toe, even your whole foot, maybe even up to your knee, in the female lineage of that same tradition. Yes, at least you, who awoke to the seduction of literature as a child through the work of Ursula K. Le Guin, understand that "male writers" and "female writers" is a bizarre and useless distinction, beneath the serious consideration of any true—which is to say open-hearted—reader.

> "I read a piece of writing and within a paragraph or two I know whether it is by a woman or not. I think [it is] unequal to me."
> —V. S. Naipaul

Does Cercas suffer from the malady Francine Prose once identified as gynobibliophobia? I suspect he does. Though if I'm honest, I must admit that I, too, suffer from this disease. Yes, I, a woman, am afraid of women's books. This is why I picked up *The Fifth Child* last weekend. I've been trying to read more novels by women, more memoirs, more poetry, more essays, more short stories. Because the fact of the matter is, if I were ever to attempt to write a book about the novel, as Cercas has done, its pages would likewise be filled with the names of male novelists simply because it is mostly male novelists I have read, and it is mostly male novelists I love and mostly male novelists I respect and admire. I hang my head in shame, sitting here at my computer as I type these words, but it's true. Am I really so lost? So disenfranchised? So confused? I'm afraid it's the case.

> *... continued (10:40 pm)*

You know, I've often wondered what it's like to be you, the person, Karl Ove Knausgaard, and not just because you're such a brilliant thinker, idiosyncratic writer, and A++ reader, but also because, in addition to these things, you are a white-skinned European male and for this reason have not an inkling of what it's like to be in a position that's essentially adjunct to both the practice and history of literature and, beyond that, humanity itself.

> "Man is defined as a human being and woman as a female."
> —Simone de Beauvoir

You wouldn't know this, not firsthand, perhaps not even secondhand, but the adjunct position is a deeply destructive place in which to reside. It can shrink you right up if you're not careful. And I, for one, am not always careful. Though back in college I was vigilant. For example, in every textbook I read, in every course packet I received, wherever the word "man" was used to indicate not a male of my own species but a human being, I carefully prefaced it with the letters *hu*. I likewise altered every "he," where it was meant to indicate a person of either sex, by placing an *s/* in front of it. And "mankind," under my pencil, became, always, "*hu*-mankind." I made these edits not as a political statement, but only in order to get through whatever I was reading, because my brain simply wouldn't allow free passage to words like "man" and "he" when they indicated (or tried to indicate) a human being. My female brain in my female body bristled at such "gender-neutral" usage because it didn't feel neutral at all. It felt quite partisan. It made me feel subsumed. Invisible. Negligible. And these feelings stoppered the reading process. In short, I made my edits simply in order to be *able* to read the work. It took a lot of time.

> "The spider is a repairer. If you bash into the web of a spider, she doesn't get mad. She weaves and repairs it."
> —Louise Bourgeois

As I grew more fully into adulthood, I no longer repaired the texts I read. I figured I had better things to do. After all, everyone knows exactly what a statement like, "One small step for man, one giant leap for mankind" is supposed to mean. Right? Why bushwhack my way through such an endless, ever-renewing onslaught of grammatical negation? Because once you start looking for these types of things, they crop up everywhere. I eventually trained myself to remain unfazed whenever I encountered this kind of language. In fact, I took pride in gliding past it—took it as a sign of my own maturity. It's only now (mature indeed), only now (with a daughter entering her twenties) that I realize this was a serious mistake.

... continued (after, happily, discovering a sleeve of ginger snaps at the back of the breadbox)

Speaking of mistakes, there's a passage early on in Book 2 that's so smug, so macho (in a literary way), that's so—*ugh!* I can't explain it. It's almost as if language repels this feeling—the one that comes over me whenever I read something like this.

All you're trying to do in this passage is one of your favorite bad boy tricks—an anti-PC rant that in this case attempts to flip the conventional nature vs. nurture argument on its head. But it's all so—testosteroney. And white. You don't really have a leg to stand on, and yet you don't even know it! You begin by invoking the name Ingmar Bergman (via the Swedish critic Sven Stolpe, via your best friend and daily conversational partner, Geir Angell), when you inform the reader that he (Bergman) once claimed that "he would have been Bergman irrespective of where he had grown up." A page later you raise the name of another Scandinavian great, Dag Solstad, whose literary style, as you describe it, is "inimitable and full of élan" and "cannot be learned ... [nor] bought for money," the idea being that Solstad's style should be taken as clear evidence of the ineffable individual essence with which each of us is endowed at birth. Your contention, ultimately, is that men like Bergman and Solstad were born geniuses and would have become exactly what we now know them to be no matter how or where or under what kind of hegemonic conditions their lives might have otherwise unfolded. You end with this: "It is not the case that we are born equal and that the conditions of life makes our lives unequal, it is the opposite, we are born unequal, and the conditions of life make our lives more equal."

What I want to know is, are you for real? I don't mean this sarcastically. I really want to know. Is this *really* what you think? I mean, don't you ever look down at your own hands as they play across the keyboard? Clackety-clack. Your own meaty, white—maybe hairy, who knows, probably soft—hands, and wonder? Just a little?

In irritation,
Kim Adrian

May 11, 2019

Dear Knausgaard,

Lisa and I both have May birthdays. Hers is the 10th, mine the 6th, so two days ago we had a small afternoon party at my place. I made miniature sandwiches, half a dozen deviled eggs, a simple Bundt cake moistened with a few spoonfuls of Madeira, and the four of us—Lisa, Shuchi (who also works at the bookstore), a new acquaintance named Nina, and myself—sat around my dining room table drinking a pot of peppermint tea and talking about a lot of things, but mostly books. At one point I mentioned to Nina that I'd just discovered a shared interest: "Lisa told me you also like Knausgaard." Nina said that actually she loves your work, especially *A Time for Everything*, the novel you wrote right before *My Struggle*. She asked if I'd read it. I told her I had, then we chatted for a little while about your almost hallucinogenic descriptions of angels in that novel, and about the Bible stories you retell, and the strangely pastoral seventeenth-century vibe of the whole thing. But as neither Lisa nor Shuchi has read this book, the conversation soon circled around to *My Struggle*.

"The thing I like best about it," Nina said, "is how incredibly attentive he is. To everything."

"Exactly," said Lisa.

"It's not that everything matters, but he pays attention to every single thing, just in case it bears meaning."

Again, Lisa said, "Exactly."

I didn't say so at the time, but I don't agree. I don't think that's what you're doing. Actually, I think you're doing the opposite. I think you're saying that things don't have to bear meaning, because meaning isn't the point. It's beside the point. What matters is simply paying attention. Or to put it another way: what matters is being alert to the state of being alive.

"It's the *way* he looks at things," said Lisa. "Because he isn't afraid to look at the ordinary and the ill-formed and the vain. He exposes all that's on the inside—all that he's experiencing inside himself as he looks at the world—and, yes, he violates a lot of social norms in order to expose those things, and many people don't want to look at what he's doing for even a minute because it's so unattractive. But that is the beauty of it."

"And yet it's problematic," I said. "Because by letting everything on the inside come out, and by being completely truthful about his feelings and perceptions, he hurts a lot of people."

"I don't get that at all," said Lisa.

"Really? I thought that was the whole point of Book 6."

Lisa and I often have mini-tiffs about your work. Basically, she's a purist, which means that when she loves something, she does so completely. I benefit from this as her friend, but it's annoying when I disagree with her. "He *had* to do it in order to live," she said. "He would have died otherwise. He *had* to be real. He *had* to fight for that kind of reality. And I admire that greatly. I would like to be that transparent. I know he kills himself on a daily basis, I mean all of us do, trying to be true, but when you set the bar that high..."

I poured myself some more tea. I always feel like a fake when Lisa talks this way. I mean, I try to live a good life. I try to be a good person. But do I examine these ideas as carefully as I should? What does "good" actually mean? And do I *really* want to be *real*, like you? Like Lisa? Is being *real* even a *good* thing? Or is it selfish? Is selfishness necessary to live in the deepest way possible, to touch life as intensely and truthfully and courageously as possible? Am I—adorer of all that is cozy, safe, and reliable, all that is tasty, all that is sweet—actually content, when everything's said and done, to sleepwalk through my allotted time on this planet? To waste huge quantities of my own limited life force simply because being real is such a lot of lonely work? These were the kinds of questions going through my mind as I ate a second slice of cake soaked, forkful by forkful, in milky peppermint tea.

Yours,
K. A.

May 26, 2019

Dear Knausgaard,

I'm sitting at a wooden table in the kitchen of a small house on a small island forty minutes by ferry off the coast of a much larger island in mid-coast Maine. It's late May and unseasonably cold. I didn't fall asleep for over an hour last night because I was so cold. My toes, even in cashmere socks, were like ice, and my fingers, even tucked under the waistband of my pajamas, were icy, too. Today, the sky is matte white everywhere but the south, where it's just the faintest bit gray and the cloud cover hugs so close to the land that the view out the window on my right reminds me of a stage set made of carefully painted scrims: a thin ribbon of road, a stretch of dune grass, a lone telephone pole, the curve of Toothacher Cove, almost black today, and beyond that, a long shelf of pink granite, a thick growth of fir trees, choppy and pointy as they'd be in a child's drawing, and finally, the low-hanging, barely gray sky.

Ever since reading *A Time for Everything* I think of you whenever I come up here, especially when I take a bath. Or, rather, let me rephrase that: I think about the final scene in *A Time for Everything* whenever I take a bath up here, because right above the tub is a window with a view directly onto the water, and this is exactly like the bathtub-window situation that Henrik Vankel remarks upon as he bathes his self-mutilated body in the final pages of that complicated novel. For years I've experienced a quietly exhilarating sense of dislocation whenever I take a bath in this house and, at the same time, gaze out over the water—which is sometimes shimmering and full of light, sometimes green and opaque, almost milky. But I hadn't understood the curious circuitry of this sensation until I read what Vankel makes of it in *A Time for Everything*:

> Wasn't there something ingenious about lying in a container full of water several feet above the ground, staring out across the sea? Whenever I thought this, I would sometimes feel a yearning, and it must be yearning in its purest form, because I never knew what I was yearning for. But I liked it; that sudden feeling of expectation, with its quivering nerves and abrupt rush of joy in the breast, was enough in itself.

In Book 1 of *My Struggle* you describe a similar sensation that arises whenever you, as a teenager, "walk through town, playing my Walkman... Something to do with the distance between the inside and the outside worlds arose then, something that I liked so much; when I saw all the drunken faces of people who had gathered by the bars it was as if they existed in a different dimension from mine..." A bit later in the same volume you write about going out onto the street with a cup of coffee in your hand. "A slight feeling of unease arose within me at seeing it out there, the cup belonged indoors, not outdoors; outdoors, there was something naked and exposed about it, and as I crossed the street I decided to buy a coffee at the 7-Eleven the following morning, and use their cup, made of cardboard, designed for outdoor use, from then on." In still another scene, you discover one snowy winter night that your father has left the garage door open. Inside the garage, you notice that the gravel underfoot is "snow-free and dry," and confess that the sight of it "aroused a faint unease" in you "because gravel belonged outdoors, and whatever was outdoors should be covered in snow, creating an imbalance between inside and outside."

The inner and the outer, the tension between what's hidden or private and what's obvious or public, not to mention the endless variety of structures and mental inventions that separate the one from the other—in many ways these concerns constitute the very heart of *My Struggle*, its core preoccupation. You spell this out quite clearly dozens, if not hundreds, of times over the course of the novel, in small incidental asides as well as larger, more clearly philosophical explorations. Toward the beginning of Book 5, for example, which covers your life as a newly matriculated student at the University of Bergen, you describe composing what you considered, at the time, a hilariously transgressive poem consisting of nothing but the word "cunt" repeated more than five-hundred times in ALL CAPS. You were, I know, only eighteen. But it's moments like these that make me think I wouldn't like you in real life. At any rate, you (or, technically speaking, Karl Ove) were quite pleased with this "poem" until you realized that you couldn't possibly share it with your writing workshop because it was too "full of hatred." It belonged, you write, in your room, where you were "all alone, not ... with other people." You then pursue a line of thought very familiar to any reader who's stuck with you from Book 1 to this point: "Of course I could break down the partition between these two worlds, but there was something very strong holding them apart, which told me they shouldn't be mixed."

Again and again you examine the qualities of this very strong something. For example, in the seasonal quartet (that string of oddly lopsided little books you wrote right after *My Struggle*), you make a careful examination of things like pipes and windows, which also serve to keep one kind of thing separate from another kind of thing. You write as well of eyes and mouths—entry and exit points from the inner to the outer. Transgressing or somehow transcending the boundary between these two states is a source of constant wonder, fear, and yearning in your work. It is also a source of great pain whenever this boundary takes the form of shame, which, like a private alarm system, or some kind of easily inflamed membrane, alerts us to our own offenses whenever a bit too much of our inner lives (where, to paraphrase you, every idiocy, every ugliness, perversity, and cruelty—every all-caps CUNT poem—can peacefully run its course) somehow manages to seep out into the larger world, at which point that emotion surges up, vibrating madly through every cell and making us want to disappear, to die on the spot, to sink into the earth and hide within it.

That you have an especially intimate relationship with shame has everything to do with your father, who instilled in you a profound appreciation of the private, inner realm by driving you deeper and deeper into it. He, who tracked your every move, your every sideways glance, even your every thought (it often seemed to you), who mocked you for your natural "effeminacy" and the fey-sounding lisp you had as a child, who was forever on the alert for any hint of what might be going on inside your head and heart.

But how did he do it? How did he always seem to know exactly what you were thinking? How could he possibly see that you were hiding candy under the covers of your bed, when the covers were *covering* the candy? All those insane scenes and fragments of scenes in which your father unleashes his own self-loathing onto you, his child, like a dog having a good piss. He's a finely tuned nut-job, your dad, alert to even the most subtle infractions: his rage, for instance, over a tiny, months-old stain of orange juice at the bottom of the kitchen wall.

That scene reminded me so much of my own childhood, a period of years during which, it seems to me now, I spent most of my time hiding. Yet it never did any good. Because my mother, like your father, had a knack for knowing exactly how to get inside my head. In fact, she often assured me she knew everything I was thinking and feeling, only better than I knew myself. And I believed her. Of course, they were only tricksters. My mother, your father. All they had to do was look in our eyes.

Kids are such open books. They have no idea. It's so beautiful.

... continued (near midnight, near the wood stove)

I realized about twenty minutes ago, lying awake in bed, too cold to sleep (despite my socks, despite my hat and scarf), that I've hardly mentioned your children, those fierce ice-cream ogres, those small bodies sprawled on the couch watching *Bolibompa*, those delicate memories in the making. So I came into the kitchen, put a log on the fire, made myself a cup of tea, and started flipping through the books.

I know for a fact, because I clearly remember, because their presence was quite vivid as I read, that Vanja, Heidi, and John flit in and out of view throughout the entirety of *My Struggle*. They're like lightening bugs: charming but elusive—and also, as I just discovered, surprisingly hard to find when you go searching for them. It took a while, but I finally ran across this fairly representative bit, in Book 6, which finds you preparing them for an outing, first by helping Heidi (who's something of a clothes horse) decide on an outfit involving Hello Kitty tights, then by dressing John, your youngest (though not before wiping his privates with a damp cloth so that he won't smell of the "faint, yet pungent, salty odor of urine left by his diaper"). There is a full paragraph concerning the difficulty of finding a matching pair of socks, though eventually you do—purple and "slightly on the feminine side." These you slip over your son's "outstretched feet." It's the word "outstretched," here, that I love, that makes John come alive on the page, no matter how briefly. You're so good at capturing, through tiny verbal gestures like this one, the mix of passivity and helpfulness, willfulness and impotence that children exude. As well as the sense that they're watching us all the time. Absorbing everything we do as they strive to outgrow precisely the same world you want so badly to recapture: I mean the world as it is for a child, one shaped by emotion and sensuous engagement with physical reality.

Throughout *My Struggle* you often note your children's efforts to leave this world behind in order to enter the one in which we adults operate: a world of clear-cut tenses and dictionary definitions, one shaped by ideas, expectations, and contexts. In Book 1, for instance, you describe your eldest child, Vanja, sitting in a café with you and Linda, chasing facts with questions: "Is the sky fixed? Can anything stop autumn coming? Do monkeys have skeletons?" In another café, in Book 6 (though referring to roughly the same time period), Vanja seems bored and grumpy. Trying to entertain her, you take an apple out of your backpack and explain that you can speak "applish." You give the fruit a shake, hold it to your ear, and translate what it says for your daughter: "What a lovely girl. What's her name?" But Vanja isn't fooled. "That was you," she says. And you feel sorry for her.

Parenting is a duplicitous act on a number of fronts, but none quite so much as this: coaxing (however reluctantly) one's children into the shackles of social life and the adult world of argument and obligation, manners, common sense, hard work, civic duty, and individual responsibility. Which means that your children's presence in *My Struggle* serves as more than simply an illustration of your engagement with the endless tasks of parenthood ("diapers that have to be changed, clothes that have to be put on, breakfast that has to be served, faces that have to be washed, hair that has to be combed and pinned up, teeth that have to be brushed, squabbles that have to be nipped in the bud, slaps that have to be averted, rompers and boots that have to be wriggled into..."), it also provides three living, breathing examples of the problem that preoccupies you most: the movement away from an embodied experience of reality and toward a more knowledgeable but essentially alienated one. This movement occurs on the individual scale through the process we call "growing up," but you perceive it as well on the scale of human history, in the sense that we, the grand-children—or perhaps the great-great-grand-children—of the Enlightenment, find ourselves living in a world composed largely of images with "no weight, no depth, no time, and no place." Images that are "nowhere and everywhere." A world of websites, television news, radio reports, and ad campaigns, of data, statistics, and margins, of selfies and GIFs, of telephone calls, magazines, books, text messages, and Zoom meetings.

It reminds me of something Camus once said, but I can't think what now. My eyes have started shutting on their own, even as I sit here. I dread the cold of the bed with its icy sheets—thirty feet away from the stove and surrounded by large black windows. Where's a hot water bottle when you need one? That's what I'd like to know.

—*Kim*

P.S. (next a.m.—slept like a rock) "A society based on symbols is, in its essence, an artificial society in which the physical truth of humankind becomes a hoax." That's the Camus quote I was thinking of. I just Googled it and up it popped.

May 30, 2019

Dear Knausgaard,

The day before I came up to Maine, I stopped by the bookstore to drop off a couple of journals Shuchi had lent me. She wasn't around, so I stood on line to give them to Paul, her boyfriend, who was working the register. Because I was in such a bad, essentially involute mood (long story), I didn't even notice Lisa standing directly in front of me. She was chatting with a customer waiting in line to pay. It was only when I saw the book this customer was buying, *What You Have Heard Is True*, by Carolyn Forché, that I thought to look more closely at the short, dark-haired woman just inches in front of me. Yes—it was Lisa. Of course it was. Carolyn Forché is her new true love and Lisa's been pressing her most recent book on everyone she knows. Sorry to say, but you have been demoted. For Carolyn Forché, Lisa has actually created a shrine, complete with twinkling lights. Well, that's how it goes. Before Forché's memoir it was Han Kang's *The White Book*, which Lisa gave me as a gift, insisting I read it for mental health purposes, actually as an antidote to you—to your work, which, if I'm frank, did rather drag me down there, at the end, and which Lisa in recent months (ever since Book 6) has come to regard as dark and oppressive, relentlessly so. But *The White Book* was not an antidote. I found it thin, pretty, but unremarkable outside of its striving melancholy—though I didn't share these impressions with Lisa, because she takes her literary crushes, no matter how fleeting they may be, incredibly seriously.

After I gave Paul the journals, and the customer ahead of me had left, Lisa and I chatted near the current releases. We talked about Rachel Cusk for a while, because her new book of essays just came out. It has a very nice cover, we agreed, po-mo in an elegant, low-key way, like the covers on the re-releases of her trilogy: *Outline, Transit,* and *Kudos*. I wish I had the new editions of those books because the covers are so good, but I have the dorky old ones instead, one of which Cusk signed a couple of months ago, when Lisa, Nina, Shuchi and I went to see her give a reading in Cambridge. Cusk was pretty much the way I expected her to be, which is to say pretty much like Faye, the protagonist of her trilogy: fragile, standoffish, graceful, intelligent, a little—bitter? I liked her. It's always fun to see an author you admire in real life—to see how their energy fills the room, or doesn't. Cusk's didn't. But that wasn't too surprising, considering her work. I mean the way she disappears into it.

I wonder what you make of Cusk's trilogy, which attempts something very similar to *My Struggle*, something like an emptying of the self or, as you put it in Reykjavik, an *obliteration* of the self, which, you told the audience that night, is what literature *is*. But Cusk goes about this task in precisely the opposite way you do. Because while you write almost exclusively about yourself—*your* perceptions, *your* thoughts, *your* feelings, *your* memories—Cusk's narrator does almost none of that. Instead, she inverts all the most basic conventions of first-person narration by merely listening to other people's stories about *their* perceptions, *their* thoughts, *their* feelings, *their* memories. Reeling from the after-effects of a painful divorce, Faye listens with incredible patience, even with—it often seems—a kind of penitence, to the stories told to her by the people she encounters in her everyday life: a man on a plane; her writing students; colleagues at a conference; an old lover; the contractor renovating her apartment...

The relationship between your work and Cusk's was the basis of a question posed, after her reading, by a man wearing a pair of self-consciously professorial wire-rimmed glasses. "Your trilogy and Knausgaard's six-volume opus, *My Struggle*," he intoned, "are both exemplars of what's popularly known as autofiction. Beyond this, in what ways would you say your work overlaps with his?" Cusk responded only by saying that she thought you had landed on your subject matter and a successful approach to it much sooner than she had landed on hers. I found it a pretty deft way to avoid putting herself in the same camp as you, which seems only fair. But it didn't give your fans a lot to chew on. Though just a bit later I was reminded of your work again, when Cusk spoke briefly about freedom. She evoked a simple image: a woman standing inside a house surrounded by her family (children, husband) looking out a window and onto the street, thinking, "That's where freedom lies." Yet, Cusk warned, when this same woman is expelled from her home and finds herself, both metaphorically and actually, on the street, it's only to find that the public sphere isn't free at all, but full of menace, precisely because she's a woman.

I thought of you when she said these things because you, too, are obsessed with the idea of freedom. You seek it on every page of *My Struggle*, both through your style, which is formless, open, rangey, and through your dogged pursuit of embodied experience, that's to say, experience unfettered, unbound by ideas, concepts, knowledge, or social constraints. You seek freedom as well in life itself (at least Karl Ove does), which is in large part what led you (that is, Karl Ove) to develop such an unhealthy relationship with alcohol ("getting drunk in the middle of the day was a good feeling, there was a lot of freedom in it, suddenly the day opened and offered quite different opportunities now that I didn't care about anything").

Lisa, also, is a passionate seeker of freedom. When she speaks of her marriage, for example (which she does often), it is usually in relation to this question of freedom. How can she be truly free, truly herself, and truly alive while remaining in her marriage, which is so full of compromises, as all marriages are? How can she pursue her own needs and desires while also attending to those of her husband and sons? It's largely on account of this element of your work—your continual quest for freedom—that Lisa admires it so much. But if I'm honest, I don't know what any of you are talking about. Not you, not Cusk, not Lisa. What is freedom? I have my whole life sought its precise opposite: security. Would I even know freedom if it leapt up and bit me on the nose? Have I ever in my life felt truly free? Have I ever in my life actually *wanted* to be free? Only when I'm at my desk. And that's an uphill thing.

> "A true work must start from the oblivion or destruction (transformation) of the writer's very self."
> —Julio Ramon Ribeyro

Well, I've got to go get some more wood. It's a bit of a trek out to the old sheep shed, where we store it, especially in the rain. But the fire needs building up.

—*Kim*

June 2, 2019

Dear Knausgaard,

Again, it's cold! June, and everything still feels brittle. Damp. At least my friend Julie is here on the island with me. She arrived yesterday and is working in the bedroom upstairs right now. I can occasionally hear her up there humming little snippets and walking around in her clogs. Maybe she's pacing as she thinks. She's a composer. She's writing the music for an opera for which I've written the libretto. My job is to be a kind of sounding board and make any changes to the text she might need as she goes along. But most of the time I don't have a lot to do.

Of course I brought up a bunch of books to read, but once I got here none of them seemed very appealing, so last night Julie lent me her copy of Christa Wolf's *The Quest for Christa T.*, which I started before going to bed. There's an interesting line in the second chapter that made me think of you. Christa T. has recently died and the narrator, her friend, has wound up in possession of her childhood diary. On the cover of this diary Christa T. wrote a long time ago, "I would like to write poems and I like stories too." The narrator ponders this phrase:

> Write poems, 'dichten,' *condensare*, make dense, tighten; language helps. What did she want to make tight, and against what did it have to be resistant?

I understand this impulse to tighten and make resistant. It's a common inclination. Writers everywhere seek to do exactly this in order to convey the essence of things, and it's a much-admired quality when done well. But you seek to do just the opposite. Instead of tightening, you loosen. Instead of reducing, you expand, open things up. "Open," in fact, is a favorite word of yours—an almost sacred touchstone. But what exactly do you mean by "open," I've often wondered? Something that isn't closed, I suppose. That's clear enough. But what does *that* mean? Something like a mouth, perhaps, or an eye? Or something full of pores, like our skin? In other words, something that lacks a definitive inside and a clear-cut outside, something permeable? Or do you mean something more straightforward, like a door swinging on its hinges?

"Come on! Into the open, my friend," Hölderlin urges you in Book 2, and your goal in *My Struggle* is to heed this advice, to follow the scent of openness, like a psycho bloodhound, wherever you run across it. In the passage immediately preceding this quote, you catch a whiff of it in Italo Calvino's *The Baron in the Trees* and in Carl-Henning Wijkmark's *The Draisine*, both of which, you explain, you read while visiting your in-laws at their house, deep in the woods. You read these books while lying in a bed where the stars were "visible through the window above, surrounded by darkness and silence." You also read Thomas Bernhard's

Extinction in this bed, but say that the experience did not provide the same "fantastic" feeling. In fact, everything in Bernhard's novel felt to you "closed off in small chambers of reflection," which, you explain, repelled you because you wanted "to be as far from that which was closed and mandatory as it was possible to be.... But how, how?" And just then, in the very next paragraph—how relieved I was to see it!—you provide the answer:

> I sat down on the chair by the window. A pot of meat broth was steaming in the middle of the table. A basket of fresh homemade rolls beside it, along with a bottle of mineral water and three cans of *folköl*, Swedish low-alcohol beer. Linda put Vanja in the baby seat at the end of the table, sliced a roll in half, gave it to her, and then went to warm up a jar of baby food in the microwave. Linda's mother took over and Linda sat down next to me.

Your answer, in other words, is your calling card, your fetish, your claim to fame—almost every reviewer has remarked upon it—your bizarrely plodding yet compelling attention to detail. Or no, not just detail. What you point to involves detail but is not limited to it; it's more like attention—to everything, all the little crumbs of life, remarkable or unremarkable as they may be. It hardly matters which, because openness, freedom, the experience of breaking though the constriction of all that is "closed and mandatory," is to be found only in immediate sensory experience and its unpredictable, ever-present shadow: emotion. Yes, only by paying attention to your own actual concrete physical encounters with that aspect (and only that aspect) of the world immediately surrounding you can you outwit your own contextualizing, conceptualizing mind and be, as you like to put it, an *idiot*. Any popular Buddhist text will reference this same idea: the pulse of life, the true vitality of life, the feeling of life unfurling constantly, though at its own slow, dark pace, is located in our actual—and only in our actual—interactions with the world and only precisely *now*. It hides everywhere, in boredom as much as in ecstasy, but it is perhaps easiest to recognize in the kinds of details we used to absorb as young children, before our minds became overgrown with abstract knowledge.

If I squint a little, I can see it, for instance, in the wood of the table on which my laptop rests as I type these words: a medium brown oak (I'm pretty sure it's oak) with hairlike striations of grayer and blonder browns running through it, all overlaid with blackish nicks and scars that have built up over perhaps a century of use. These look in some places like manic bird scratchings and in others like thin crescent moons. On this table there's a little bowl of salt and I can see it there, too, in the tiny grains that are curiously unluminous, like dry, very fine granular snow. I'm pretty good with detail but not as good as you, so I'll embarrass myself no further. I'm just saying that I recognize, in part because of your many reminders, that it's here—all around me and also inside me. It is, perhaps especially, where what's around me and what's inside me intersect, which is unpinpointable because I am in fact open, or at least porous. I can feel this porousness in my right foot, which I've had crossed over my left leg for so long it feels almost drunk, woozy after its extended conversation with gravity. I can also feel it in the burn on my left forefinger—a tough, linear, white blister about an inch long—which I got earlier today while feeding a log to the stove and stupidly pulling the lid shut with my bare hand instead of using a rag. I can feel it in my sinuses as well, which are swollen (I have a cold), and in my nose with every breath, especially my right nostril, which is clearer than the left and which feels a little raw as I draw the air—which I cannot see, but which I trust implicitly—into my lungs before releasing it once more into the world.

As always,
K. A.

June 6, 2019

Dear Knausgaard,

Last night I had a funny dream about Rachel Cusk that involved a purse, which I found curious, as well as some difficulty around making a connecting flight. I don't often dream about writers. Not that I remember, anyway. Though once, a long time ago, I did have a nice dream about Seamus Heaney and some geraniums. And Mary Karr, a few years back, gave me a small and extremely sweet orange in a dream. But about you I've had two dreams. In the most recent, just a couple of weeks ago, I saw your face in three-quarters profile, almost as if you were posing for a photograph, which makes sense, since you always seem to be posing for photographs. But you weren't, you were just sitting there, or maybe standing. In any case, it seemed clear you felt yourself unobserved because your features were so neutral, neither happy nor sad, despite the fact that a line of tears ran slowly from your left eye down your slightly sagging cheek and from there into the gray thatch of your beard. What's curious about this dream, I think, is how my subconscious mind was quoting you even as I slept because I know I've read—somewhere—something you once said about how tears are an outer expression of an inner state: a kind of leaking from the inside to the out.

The other dream was from the summer before last and it was more complicated. I was napping, and in my sleep I could hear the kids on the basketball court in the schoolyard next door. Their voices and the dream mingled together tenaciously. I tried but couldn't pull them apart. I felt a little panicked, yet it was also kind of intoxicating, actually really delicious to feel so lost, to not know which way to turn in order to wake up. The window was wide open. It was warm outside. A perfectly beautiful summer afternoon. The air smelled like gently simmering chlorophyll. A boy was calling my son's name. "Jonaaaaah! Jonaaaaah!" In the dream I could sense not only the warmth of the sunshine, the softness of the air, but also the presence of my own childhood. Or maybe it was your childhood? I was in the middle of reading Book 3 at the time, and when this boy, one of my son's best friends, called out my son's name, his voice got muddled with your voice—that's to say, his voice got muddled with the voice of the child named Karl Ove that you project onto the pages of Book 3. This boy, whose name is Senya, is Russian. He is fierce and blond and troublesomely alpha, but also sweet. For instance, once Jonah fell down and hurt his leg when he and a bunch of friends were doing parkour on the playground. It was Senya who scooped him up and carried him over to a bench, asking the whole time if he was all right. And it was this boy's voice, slightly ragged with the beginnings of puberty, that I heard as I struggled to exit the dream. *Jonaaaaah!* Senya's voice, my son's name: the two children overlapped seamlessly in my mind. At exactly the same time, this Senya-Jonah entity overlapped, as I've just explained, with the eleven-year-old boy named Karl Ove, and, beyond that, the eleven-year-old Karl Ove overlapped with the eleven-year-old me, about whom I had forgotten, completely forgotten, a long time ago, but who had recently risen to the surface as I'd lost myself in the pages of the book that lay open on the bed next to me. It was so painful—the longing I felt as I struggled between these different layers of dream and reality, of past and present. I awoke with a sob.

... continued (11:30 a.m.)

Julie and I just took a break together (decaf tea and seedy, whole grain health bars infused with Omega 3 oils ☹) during which Julie sang, while facing away from me (because she was embarrassed), two newly composed lines from our opera, one of which sent shivers up and down my spine and not only because it was such a beautiful string of sounds, but because in putting the words I'd written to music, she'd animated them in a way I hadn't expected. They seemed, suddenly, to have a shape, and that shape orbited around itself. I thought, for some reason, of three interlocking triangles. It was surprising.

Now she's back upstairs, pacing and humming, and I'm sitting here in the kitchen thinking about some of your more persistent preoccupations, jotting them down, trying to sort them out. I've come up so far with:

- the inner vs. the outer
- biological life vs. material reality
- freedom vs. responsibility
- the heart vs. the mind

Time might count as a fifth, but I'm on the fence. Your treatment of it, though often exciting, feels almost gestural. I mean, I could practically see you thinking about Proust a lot of the time. Not that that wasn't interesting—it was, I'm just saying I'm not sure time really counts as a thing for you. Speaking of Proust, as Julie and I were hiking in the woods yesterday, Julie (who's finally given in and started reading Book 1) said she'd noticed a long paragraph near the beginning of that volume in which you describe your grandmother's garden in a manner that reminded her of *Swann's Way*. It made her wonder if this was something people say about you, that you're kind of like a modern-day, Norwegian, rock 'n' roll style Proust? I had to laugh, because of course people say this about you all the time. People who pay attention to you, that is. Which, if you listen to the hype sometimes seems like everybody, yet this is hardly the case. Julie, for instance, although a very engaged reader, hadn't heard of you until I started talking her ear off about *My Struggle* last year. This is something I find strange: how hugely you loom on the literary scene, with articles and reviews about your work and, often, profiles of your personal life appearing in every corner of the internet, in many of the biggest print publications, and countless smaller ones, not to mention on legions of personal blogs, and yet only a handful of the people I know personally have actually read your work. Many friends and acquaintances have never even heard of you, and I know some pretty well-read people. On top of that, a lot of your most ardent admirers seem to have stalled somewhere around Book 4 or 5. Even my friend Bill, who's written a short monograph about *My Struggle*, hadn't yet picked up Book 6 the last time I talked to him. And my friend Nina, who, as I've mentioned, loves your work, stopped reading with Book 4. Even Lisa—Lisa!—didn't one-hundred-percent finish Book 6, opting to skip over the Hitler essay, because, as she put it, "it just doesn't belong."

At first I agreed with her on this, and for a long time afterwards I still agreed. I thought it was odd, how shoved-in that essay felt. In the middle of a book about you and your struggle to write something "exceptional" while juggling the responsibilities of being both a good father and a decent husband, 400 pages about Hitler and your reading of *Mein Kampf*: you've got to admit, it's a little weird. But now, a year later, I feel somehow that it's settled in my mind; that essay makes sense where it is! Not that I think it really works—all of Book 6 kind of doesn't work. I mean, it doesn't do what you say you wanted it to do, which is to *open* things, to prove somehow that the world is not limited, not closed, not finite and essentially knowable, but instead unendingly generative and full of mystery. No, Book 6 does quite the opposite.

From here, at the little table I mentioned the other day, I can see the same body of water that I can see from the bathtub. It's called Back Cove and along its edge stands a line of birch trees shimmering in the sun. On the opposite side of the field, near the road, there are three large fir trees decorated with lime-green nubbins of new needle growth and thousands of tiny male pine-cones. Every so often, a huge bisque-colored sigh of pollen will float away from these and sail across the road. Much nearer, in fact right outside the kitchen window, I can hear a bird whose song is nearly identical to that line from *Rigoletto*, "la donna è mobile," but with an extra half-syllable slipped in. Julie and I have been trying to capture this bird's song on our phones all week, without success. We head back to Boston tomorrow. I still have so much more to say. But right now, the breeze—

—K. A.

June 14, 2019

Dear Knausgaard,

Are you by any chance familiar with the work of Humberto Maturana, the Chilean biologist and philosopher? I first learned about him in my twenties, when I took a psychology class called "Family Narratives" at Harvard, where I was not a student but an employee, and where, as one of my benefits, I was allowed to take three or four classes a year at a steep discount. The professor of this class was a short, intense woman who spoke with great passion about her subject even though her head barely peeped above the podium. I filled two notebooks with scribbled quotes from her lectures, and for years afterwards I would regularly leaf through these because their pages sustained something in me. A few months ago I threw out a bunch of old paperwork, including those notebooks, which, when I last looked at them, no longer seemed to communicate anything very crucial, even though back when I was taking that class, and for so long afterwards, I counted them among my most valued possessions because they addressed the intersection of the two things that oppressed me most at the time: family and narrative.

We read Maturana's work as part of this psychology course for his theory of "autopoiesis," which had been co-opted by the field of family therapy on account of its metaphorical implications in the realm of human social—particularly familial—interactions. The basic contours of this theory share much in common with solipsism, but with an interesting twist.

Like solipsism, autopoiesis stipulates that every living being is a 100% autonomous entity, completely separate from all other aspects of existence, including, needless to say, all other autonomous entities (living beings). Isolated in this way, each human being creates not an image nor a projection of the world, but the world *itself*, at least as it manages to manifest through those operations we call the senses. Maturana, being a biologist, pays very close attention to these—the senses, or, to put it slightly more technically, he pays close attention to those biological apparatuses of perception separately owned and operated by each and every autonomous living entity. I remember the example of a dragonfly being used to illustrate the importance of physical, biological differentials when it comes to such apparatuses, because the eyes of the dragonfly couldn't be more different than ours; they feature tens of thousands of facets and sit more or less like two glittering black half-globes on the dragonfly's knobby little head, absolutely gargantuan in comparison to the rest of the insect's needle-like body. On top of this, the dragonfly's eyes see more colors than ours do, and in a weirdly segmented way. For these reasons, the world appears to be a very different place to the dragonfly than it does to you or me; it appears, in short, more dragonfly-ish. It's essential to note, however, that the dragonfly-ish world is in no way a perversion or degradation of the human-ish world, and the human-ish world is in no way closer to nor further away from the world itself than the dragonfly-ish world is because there is no such thing as the "world itself," no baseline, stable, unchanging reality lurking beneath the clashing relativism of trillions upon trillions of individual perspectives.

Where Maturana's thinking departs from straight-up solipsism is, if I remember correctly, when he stipulates that, despite the perfect autonomy of each living entity, there are countless ways in which an autonomous form may be altered *through interactions* with every other element of what we call reality.

Some of these interactions are obvious: for instance, a mother nursing her infant, or a splinter piercing the skin, or a downpour flooding a field. But others are quite subtle, almost imperceptibly so. For example, when I bought Richard Powers' novel *The Overstory* a couple of months ago, seduced in part by the cover (which really is stunning) and in part by the rave reviews and big awards, I found myself irritated within only a couple of pages by its faux mythic vibe and wound up returning the book the very next day. This was the result (Maturana would say) of my biological entity's limited ability, for whatever reason, to interact with that particular artifact produced by that particular biological entity known as Richard Powers. On the other hand, when I picked up Valeria Luiselli's newest novel, *Lost Children Archive*, shortly afterwards, and experienced exactly the opposite sensation—the familiar but always slightly thrilling tug of curiosity or desire—this also was the result of my own personal biological structure, which, for whatever reason, just so happens to be better equipped to interact with and appreciate that particular artifact of that particular biological structure known as Valeria Luiselli. If you take this reasoning just a bit further, it becomes clear that when I read an entire book, such as *It*, for example, by Inger Christensen (which happens to be the last book I read), my biological entity is altered, no matter how invisibly, by that experience, so that by the end of the book I am actually structured in a slightly different way than I was when I first opened it.

But why did I bring up Maturana in the first place? I'm not a hundred percent sure. I think he must have been skulking in the back of my mind for a while, probably since reading Christensen, because she also has very interesting views on biology. She says language *is* biology. How thrilling it was to read that. Not that I understand what it means. How can language be biology? I can't figure it out. I mean, I have a feeling about it, a gut feeling, which is kind of like a clue, but it's only a clue. Trying to hash it out in more explicit terms doesn't get me very far. For instance, it's pretty clear that my brain is a biological object, and so is my mouth and so is my tongue, and so are both of my hands, and so are my ears, and it is with these parts of myself that I produce and receive language, so, *ergo*, as they say. Frankly, it's not as crisp a thought as I'd like it to be. Basically, I'm still chewing on a lot of *It*. In any case, simply reading that line—merely brushing up against the thought of language *being* biology—was exhilarating.

Hoping this finds you well,
Kim

June 24, 2019

Dear Knausgaard,

Sometimes the ways you use the words "feminine" and "effeminate" make me feel bad. By bad, I mean deflated. As if somebody had knocked the air out of me. There are countless offhand comments about these qualities running through the entirety of *My Struggle*, and I know why. You make it clear. It has to do with your father, who was, in your view, at least when you were growing up, a "real" man, while in his eyes, as he continually reminded you, you were a bit of a joke in the testosterone department. Even your father's urine, as you describe it in Book 6, was "masculine," which is to say "dark yellow, almost brown … frightening." While yours, as a child, was "pale, almost colorless … feminine." But what does that even mean? It's not that I don't know. I know exactly what it means, but my God, *pale and almost colorless*—that sounds like something without substance—yet you equate it with *feminine*.

Elsewhere you write that once your father had divorced your mother, remarried, and become something of a hippy, he suddenly inhabited a world that struck you as "formless, uncertain, almost feminine."

Another example: on the way to your father's funeral,

in Book 1, at the airport, you carry your heavy suitcase by the handle because you detest "tiny wheels, first of all because they were feminine, thus not worthy of a man," and secondly because "they suggested easy options, shortcuts, savings, rationality, which I despised and opposed wherever I could... Why should you live in a world without feeling its weight?" And still another: in Book 2 you describe walking "around Stockholm's streets, modern and feminized, with a furious nineteenth-century man inside me." My marginalia at this point reads simply, "yuck."

If I wanted to get bummed out, I could scour your books and easily retrieve a hundred examples along these same lines. But I do not want to get bummed out. I'll say only this: the instance that galled me most, that wounded me most deeply, was, for some mysterious reason, relatively minor. It occurred on page 212 of *Winter*, the second volume of your seasonal quartet, in which you muse on a random, wide-ranging assortment of things in the world. One of these happens to be buses and in this passage you spend most of your time comparing old buses to modern ones. Old buses, you write, were "almost like boxes," while new ones are more like "gently rolling cruise ships." Old buses, you say,

> ... were different on the inside, too, for while today's buses, with their comfortable seats and elaborate interiors, often in dark colours, resemble living rooms, the interiors of buses back then were more like outhouses or sheds. And while today's buses are quiet, then they were filled with the rumbling drone of their engines, which made everything rattle and shake... The 70s were the last robust

decade. Why the decades that followed became more and more finely tuned is difficult to say, but it may simply have been that the tender souls of the 70s, the ones who sat pale and feminine in their seats staring out at the snow-covered landscape and dreaming of being far away from the roaring engines, the rattling seats and the jeering boys… were far more numerous than anyone could have imagined.

I was so with you on this—up to a point (I'm sure you can guess which one). You really nailed something, as you so often do, some ineffable thing, in this case the weird shift in contemporary Western societies toward a kind of frailty, a demand for comfort and convenience at all costs. Personally, I've always blamed Martha Stewart for this tilt toward daintiness and color coordination, but of course it's a much broader problem than that. What I'm saying is, I, too, have wondered about the way things have become more brittle, shiny, and ersatz compared to the way I remember them from my childhood, when rust was a regular feature of life—it was everywhere—and things generally just seemed a lot grittier and more bumptious. But that phrase, "pale and feminine," ripped me right out of the text. I somehow managed to scrawl the words "fuck you" next to them before throwing the book at the wall at the foot of my bed, where it fell to the floor and stayed, neither forgotten nor forgiven, for weeks.

This may sound like an overreaction. It is not. The misuse of the word feminine is a serious matter with grave consequences for people like me, which is to say, people of the female stripe. Honestly, it felt almost as if I'd been slapped in the face when I read those words. Words written by you. You, to whom I'd dedicated so much of my reading life that year, so much of my brain space, so many of my thoughts and feelings, not to mention so many of my conversational contributions when talking with all the most precious people in my life. Even my kids were sick of you!

Kim Adrian

P.S. Last summer, when I was still upset about that passage in *Winter*, my sister said something interesting. She always sees things so clearly. *Little Miss Negative Capability*. Do you know those books? The little Miss and Mister books? They're very popular here. Anyway, we were walking along a country road—just us and the apple trees, a few bees—when I mentioned how upset I was about your use of the word "feminine" in conjunction with the sleek, puffy, almost anesthetized comfort of modern public transport. I raged against your mindless sexism. But Stephanie didn't have the reaction I expected her to have. She simply patted my back and said, "I feel your pain, sis, but he's right. Buses are more feminine now. And so they should be. I'd rather have a fat, puffy bus with a hydraulic lift that lets old people and people with disabilities on and off than a rattling, beat-up one that makes some tough guy feel cool. That *is* a feminine prerogative."

June 27, 2019

Dear Knausgaard,

Somewhere in the first meaty third of Book 6, Geir Angell visits you in your Malmö apartment with his young son, Njaal. Both your wife and his are out of town, so it's just the two of you and the four kids. You make a dinner of boiled sausages, which split in the water, and which the children eat while watching television in the living room while you and Geir eat and talk in the kitchen. In the overall chronology of the larger narrative, this section, though near the novel's end, takes place just as Book 1 is about to hit the shelves. Waves of anguish and anxiety overtake you almost continually because of the legal actions your paternal uncle, Gunnar, keeps threatening over what he considers the many lies that fill your account of the circumstances surrounding your father's death, an event you cover in great detail in Book 1. You've been obsessing over these troubles, but Geir's presence helps you forget them for a while.

Geir cuts a curious figure in *My Struggle*. He's almost a second brother to you, though he's many other things as well: fellow Norwegian ex-pat living in Sweden, patient sounding board, reliable pep-talker, devil's advocate, informal editor, daily conversational partner, marital commiserator, confessor, and, above all, muse. "Muse" is such a gendered term—and gendered in such complex ways—that I hesitate to use it here, but Geir does regularly inspire you, even when you don't notice it. For example, earlier that same day—the split sausages day—he reminds you that it was he who first suggested the title *My Struggle*. "Seriously?" you ask.

> "It was in a sentence you said, my struggle, and I said there you go, there's your title. That's how it was."
>
> "Shit."
>
> "It's how you work. Your head's this simmering pot, everything goes into the soup."

A little later that same evening, as the four children, all very young, splash around in the bathtub together while you and Geir keep watch over them, you begin a long internal monologue regarding the relationship of individual sensibility to artistic output. These thoughts are initiated by reflections on your best friend; you meditate briefly on Geir's childhood, his parental relationships, and his time in Iraq, where he'd travelled years earlier to act as a human shield in the Gulf War. Since his return, he's been submerged in an enormous writing project concerning that experience, and as the two of you spend so much time at your respective desks, your lives, you write, "had become almost parodically similar, everything was suddenly about what we were doing in our little rooms, practically cut off from the rest of the world apart from our families. I read what he wrote, he listened to me reading out loud what I wrote, but the relationship was not symmetrical." You say so because you consider

Geir an independent thinker, while you, you insist (a little too often), are more like a sponge. No, you're a stockpot—Geir got it right; your mind works in a more stew-like way. Something alchemical happens in there.

This essay-within-a-scene (one of your favorite maneuvers) expands still further; in fact, you let the children sit in the tub another twenty pages or so as you explore the subtle gradations between literary influence, imitation, and plagiarism. The gist of your inquiry runs like this: How does one allow for influence, which is not only necessary but inevitable, without destroying or obscuring originality? All artistic fields, you argue, demand of their practitioners a singular perspective, but none quite so much as literature, where, in your view, the "literary I" is essentially indistinguishable from the personal, innermost I—the locus for all our most private thoughts and feelings. And yet, as you put it in what may be my favorite line in all of My Struggle, "We are permeated by others." Meaning, your "literary I" has been marinating in countless other "literary I's" for decades. Specifically, you write, you've been "Gombrowiczized... Larssonized, Proustized, and Célinized, if not to say quite Sandemosial and thoroughly Hamsunified."

These authors and your thoughts on them have by this point been articulated several times in the preceding pages of My Struggle, so I don't remember if this list struck me especially as I read it, only that by the time I'd reached this point in Book 6, I was hyper-aware of your relationship to the literary canon, because books are such an integral part of the fabric of your life, and so, naturally enough, literary references, insights, and analyses crowd the pages of My

Struggle just as they crowd your thoughts.

Most of these references, insights, and analyses are, for obvious reasons, attached to the work of male writers. This is not necessarily an act of sexism on your part, but mostly a reflection of things as they are, literature as it is. Or rather as it has been until the advent of late-stage capitalism and widely available birth control.

> "Men have every advantage of us in telling their own story. Education has been theirs in so much higher a degree; the pen has been in their hands."
> —Jane Austen

But how strange it was for me, a woman, to read about the way you view yourself in relation to the canon, which is to say, as a kind of contender. For instance, late in Book 6, you reveal the genesis—the secret kernel of aspiration and inspiration—that led you to write *My Struggle* in the first place: you were sitting on the balcony of a cheap hotel in the Canary Islands late at night, Linda and the children asleep inside as you read the diaries of Witold Gombrowicz, overwhelmed with admiration for the work ("reading Gombrowicz was humiliating, the standard was so high"), yet not uncritical of it ("If he had ... described all the circumstances from which his thoughts—and through them his soul—rose, and in practice connected the highest ... with the lowest ... he would have been the world's greatest writer, the modern-day Cervantes and Shakespeare, all rolled into one. But he couldn't. He was free in thought but not in form, not quite."). And then—I picture you tipping back onto the hind legs of your chair, glancing up at the moon, taking an especially deep drag off your cigarette—you wonder: "Could I?"

This is just one instance of many that crop up in the pages of *My Struggle* which make clear how you view the canon itself not simply as a tradition of work, and not even as a direct lineage, but as an invitation, a personal challenge, a gauntlet thrown. It was strange, almost dislocating, for me to see this attitude so up close, in such detail, since you're just as unsparing in the revelations of your own, often ugly, ambition as you are with every other aspect of your life. Because the way you see yourself in relation to the canon couldn't be further from my experience. And not because I'm so humble. I'm not. It's just that when I think of "the canon" I picture a scene—it's cartoony, but that's how it goes. Scattered across a large fairground setting are many performers: all of them astonishing, though none of them are writing. They're doing circus tricks. Whatever. There are countless male performers, but only a handful of women, and as these work mostly in the shadows it's hard to see them. In fact nearly impossible. Though Sappho does have a little spotlight off in one corner. And near her, on a bed of silk, stretches Murasaki Shikibu. Then nothing—just Jane Austen's foot in a satin slipper, the back of Emily Dickinson's dark dress, an oblique glimpse of Virginia Woolf's mousey brown hair, but honestly that could be anybody. I'm not in the audience. My ego's not that crippled. No, I'm more like an energetic little rat skirting the edges of the ring, looking for something.

... continued (5 p.m.)

In Iceland, James and I bought a copy of *Egil's Saga* at an insanely overpriced tourist shop in Bogarnes. For a couple of months, James read a few pages of this book to me each night. My husband's voice, though one of the sounds I love most in the world, is like a drug. When he reads to me in bed, it takes only a couple of paragraphs, tops, before I drop off. In other words, I missed a lot of *Egil's Saga*. But I remember this: the first part of the book is essentially an annotated genealogical list that establishes Egil, the great Viking warrior, as the descendant of a long line of great Viking warriors—their rightful heir.

My favorite character in *Egil's Saga* is not Egil himself (who is both creepy and terrifying, but also mordant and tragic), but his brave nanny, Thorgerd Brak, who at one point admonishes Egil's father, Skallagrim, after he's lost a contest and, being a sore loser, kills one of his competitors, a young man named Thord, a friend of his son. Skallagrim then focuses his murderous energy on Egil, just twelve years old.

"You're attacking your own son like a mad beast!" shouts Brak. Skallagrim, taking her point, turns away from his child and levels his rage at her instead, chasing the woman off a cliff and into the sea, where she begins swimming away. But Skallagrim gets the better of her yet by heaving an enormous boulder at her back. It strikes Brak right between the shoulder blades and she sinks into the dark water, never to be seen again.

There is a monument to Thorgerd Brak in Bogarnes on the edge of what is supposed to be the very cliff she flew off of, not far from the tourist center where we bought *Egil's Saga* with the assistance of a helpful young man who told us that of all the Icelandic sagas, Egil's was his favorite. Now I know why. Once you get past the genealogy section, it's colorful stuff. And Egil himself has a nicely twisted sense of humor that often surfaces at the most brutal moments. Though the saga I really would like to have read is Thorgerd Brak's. I would have liked to know all the stories attached to her foremothers, and also how Brak herself was raised, and how it was she came to be a bondswoman, and how she felt—I mean how she perceived her own mind and body in space and time—as she raised the son of her future murderer. Unfortunately, no such saga exists. Thorgerd Brak is merely a curious fragment of *Egil's Saga*. A short tangent, tenuously adjunct to the main story.

—*Kimberli Elizabeth Adrian*

July 1, 2019

Dear Knausgaard,

Yesterday Lisa and I walked to the second best bakery in town, waffled a bit, bought nothing, walked back to the bookstore. As we strolled along the quiet residential streets of Brookline, heavily shaded by Norway maples and towering sycamores, I mentioned that I might be getting close to finishing these letters to you, and also that I was worried because there's still so much I haven't said. For instance, this annoying nebula of half-formed thoughts that's been hovering just out of reach since late April. I tried to sketch the contours of this elusive construct in the soft, humid air between us as we walked, but it was choppy.

"It has to do with Platonic ideals, and what he does in the seasonal books—what I think he does—which I know you don't agree with, but. It also has to do with the relationship of ideology to literature. Patriarchy, basically. The way it's built into language. Grammar. And his relationship to the literary canon, which is totally embedded in that structure. I mean patriarchy."

Lisa seemed a little bored, to be honest. It was so hot we kept bumping into each other. It wasn't on purpose, but it happened a lot.

"Don't worry about all that stuff," she said. "It doesn't matter. None of it matters. The only thing that matters is his gaze."

She often uses this term, "gaze," when referring to your work. She means the way you look at things, the quality of your perception, which she says is full of discipline.

> "To see clearly is poetry, prophecy, religion, all in one."
> —John Ruskin

You, too, use this word, "gaze." Or, rather, the priest who presides over your father's funeral uses it. "One must fasten one's gaze," he says.

> He could have said the little things are important; but he didn't. He could have said that loving thy neighbor is most important of all; but he didn't. Nor did he say what that gaze must be fastened upon. All he said was that it must be fastened.
>
> It made sense to me then, as we sat in the chapel and wept that morning ... and it makes sense to me today, as I sit here writing these words. I know what it means to see something without fastening one's gaze. Everything is there, the houses, the trees, the cars, the people, the sky, the earth, and yet something is missing because their being there means nothing. It could just as well be something else that was there or nothing at all. This is what the meaningless world looks like. And we can inhabit the meaningless world quite adequately, it being a simple matter of endurance...

Your descriptions in *My Struggle* are often called "granular," which is a curious word. But it does a good job of pointing to the way you attend to even the tiniest of details, and the way these details proliferate, piling up on each other, so that the world you present feels incredibly textured. Almost endless. Almost real.

And yet, as with everything in *My Struggle*, such a tricky novel, your *granular* descriptions aren't there just because they're so nifty—so nearly miraculous; they're there because they illustrate your larger philosophical intention, since it's only in the particular, the precisely local, the truly specific, that, as you put it so well, "reality's chunky solidity" resides.

Given all this, what you do in the seasonal quartet—those four vaguely autistic-seeming books you wrote after *My Struggle*—is strange. Because while these books, too, are filled with countless details, you could never call them "granular." Instead, they're a bit glassy, hard to hold onto, especially in those portions of *Autumn*, *Winter*, and *Summer* that consist of miniature *portraits* of things: apples, wasps, plastic bags, teeth, salt, foam, tears, and so on. Every one of these miniature portraits stands isolated as a kind of testament to a single, discrete facet of the world. It's almost as if you were trying to get at the *essence* of each thing, to illuminate the Platonic ideal of it; and a Platonic ideal, of course, is more or less the inverse of "reality's chunky solidity." This is what I've tried to convince Lisa of many times, but she says I'm off track. She says each mini-essay in that quartet should be read as a kind of psalm. Maybe she's right. But I still think it's weird. Weird how, for instance, in *Autumn*, you describe the mouth as being "made up of the lips, two relatively long and narrow pads which lie horizontally against eachother [sic] on the forward-facing side of the head, in the lower part of the face, below the nose..." And how in *Winter* you describe the moon as an "enormous rock" that at times "appears to be far away, like a small, distant ball," and at other times seems quite close, as when it "hangs suspended like a large luminous disc right above the treetops." Or how you define a chair as something meant "for sitting on," a thing that "consists of four legs upon which rests a board, and from the end of this rises a backrest," the whole contraption being "for one person, and one person only, which is an essential aspect of its character."

The seasonal books are addressed to your fourth child, as yet unborn when you begin the project. Your ostensible aim in them is to communicate various aspects of the world she will soon enter into. It's such an odd exercise. You, who worked so tirelessly and diligently to alert your readers, in the pages of *My Struggle*, to the critical difference between ideas and sensation, between information and experience, between knowledge and emotion, suddenly step, figuratively speaking, into the barely emergent trickle of your daughter's not-quite-life in order to introduce her to a wide and fairly random array of things in the world. Over the course of all four books, you provide her with an enormous amount of information, all of it fairly abstract, much of it well before she's even had a chance to sniff the air. I know those books are on some level meant as a gesture of welcoming, a father's anxious love letter to his unborn daughter, but they felt selfish to me. Or at least short-sighted. *Let the poor kid experience apples (teeth .... mosquitoes ... frogs ... piss ... blood ... ice cream ... eggs ...) for herself!* I kept thinking. *In her own time! On her own steam! Get out of the way, man.*

—K. A.

July 6, 2019

Dear Knausgaard,

It's insanely hot here today. The park next door is silent. Even the birds are eerily quiet. This makes for an interesting counterpoint to the book I'm reading—Bernadette Mayer's *Midwinter Day*: a book-length poem about a single day—December 22, 1978—in the life of the mother and poet named Bernadette Mayer. Mayer herself describes it as a "desirous essay on art and home." Given that, I'm sure you won't find it surprising that *Midwinter Day* often reminds me of *My Struggle*—in particular the way Mayer moves through the tasks of parenthood (dressing her daughters, taking them to the library, changing their diapers, shopping for groceries, trundling them home again) while simultaneously grappling with thoughts on art, the history and production of poetry, and the true purpose of "reading and writing." This non-stop stream of thought is studded with—pierced by—the solidity of life: taking off the little ones' winter coats, opening a wedge of cheese, drinking half a beer with a friend, "getting the dumb objects out of the bag" and dealing with "the awful sink." Thoughts flow around all of these actions and objects, like a river in which Mayer wades, sometimes up to her neck, even as she helps her children over the icy streets of Lenox, Massachusetts, reads them *The Three Little Pigs* and *Big Dog, Little Dog* and *The Tiny Tawny Kitten*, or guides them up the stairs in their clunky winter boots. It's super beautiful.

It was my sister-in-law, Julie, who turned me onto Mayer. Julie's a poet. She and I have a lot in common, I mean beyond the fact that we're both mothers and writers. For instance, we both like to knit and to bake and to garden. Actually, it's for these very reasons, and a few others, that we've been, over the years, fervidly if furtively competitive with one another. But as we've gotten older, we've both managed, somehow, to mellow, and now we're friends again, the way we were back in college, when we used to take writing workshops and dance classes together, before I started dating James. Julie teaches at the University of Colorado, so we don't get to see each other that often, but the last time she visited Boston, she and I had an interesting conversation about *My Struggle*. It started with a question: Why had I chosen to write about it? I noticed a dubious expression on her face as she asked this. It made me wonder if she didn't like *My Struggle*, because, as I'm sure you've noticed, a lot of people don't, simply as a matter of course, on principle, even if they haven't read it. I suspect it's the covers. It could also be the title. Or just the way it sounds in summary. In any case, Julie told me that she actually *had* read Book 1 and the first half of Book 2, as well, and that while she'd appreciated the writing (especially those passages that describe the physical operations of raising young children), she'd had to put it down when she got fed up with hearing you complain about how hard it is to be a father while also trying to write. Here she made another face, which clearly meant, *Try being a woman*. She got especially fed up, she said, of you acting as if you were doing your wife a huge favor every time you watched the kids. I tried to defend you—I mean the you of your novel—by explaining that Linda is mentally ill, and that as a result you (that is, Karl Ove) wind up doing the lion's share of the housework and perhaps more than your fair share of the childcare as well. Julie said "*hm*." She hadn't realized this, which is reasonable, as you don't make it clear until very late in the game, not explicitly. We were eating pre-dinner appetizers in my in-laws' kitchen as we spoke—Julie every once in a while popping a wasabi pea into her mouth, while I made steady progress on a wedge of melting brie. Eventually—it seemed inevitable—we got onto the question of whether or not *My Struggle* would have been greeted by the same fanfare had it been written by a woman. This is a much-debated point, as I'm sure you know, although it's never made a lot of sense to me. I mean, how could a woman have written *My Struggle* when *you* wrote *My Struggle*? I just don't understand the exercise of conjuring, as Katie Roiphe did in her essay "Her Struggle," a "Carla Olivia Krauss," in order to try to imagine how critics and readers might have responded to an equally gigantic novel penned by a female doppelgänger, a novel treating all the same things you treat in yours: the beauty and tedium of raising young children; the trials of intimacy and marriage; the haunting torment of a psychologically abusive parent; the textures of daily life; and, of course, the passion, vanity, and spiritual pressure that underlie all serious literary endeavors.

"It makes no sense," I said. "Every word of *My Struggle* is sifted through Knausgaard's sensibility, which acts like a filter. This filter is really the entire point of the whole thing: the specificity of one individual's *individual* experience. The power of the particular, the precisely this, here, now. The reality of a singular, local perspective."

"Yeah, maybe," said Julie. "But I think the more important point is that a woman wouldn't have gotten the same accolades for a similar book because a woman wouldn't have written a book like that in the first place. A woman wouldn't dare."

"What do you mean?"

"A woman would never take up that much room."

"What about *Miss MacIntosh, My Darling*? Or Ferrante?"

"I mean she wouldn't take up that much room and devote it entirely to *her own experience*. It's inconceivable. We're trained out of egoism to such a degree, and from such an early age, I don't even think it would be mentally possible. But it's true, if a woman did manage to write something like that, it wouldn't in a million years get the same reception. It would just be considered repulsive. Not heroic."

This is such an interesting thought, one that's stayed with me. What is it exactly that makes *My Struggle* heroic? Because as much as you may resist the notion (or at least pretend to resist it), when all is said and done, it *is* a hero's journey. And although I suspect you'd balk at the idea, if only for decorum's sake, you yourself (I'm talking about both of you: author and character) actually are heroic. Even long before the fame kicked in, you were larger than life—smarter, more articulate, better-read, simply more capable on several counts than your average Joe. And then you dug down, as deeply as you could, to reveal your thoughts and feelings, not as they "ought to be," but as they really were, and this exercise laid you (and those around you) quite bare. In this state you sought contact with something we all know but for some reason fear. I think of it as a kind of filament running through everything—a kind of energy or electricity. And it's this that really makes you extraordinary. Because not many people can do that—touch that. Some can. Not many. Bernadette Mayer can do it, and did do it in *Midwinter Day*. But that book is not a hero's journey. It's a sly, beautiful reckoning. What accounts for the difference? Is it simply a matter of scope? Of page count? Does the physical enormity of your project make it, by default, an epic, while the brevity of Mayer's renders hers a lyric? Maybe. Or is Julie right that only a man could successfully have written about these issues at such incredible length? If so, what does that mean? I mean, what does that *really* mean? And if not, if the mythical creature called Carla Olivia Krauss somehow did manage to buck all the social conventions you bucked (though skewed, of course, to accommodate the constraints inherent in being a woman rather than a man), and was able to write with as much raw, rushed beauty as you did for a few thousand pages, would Julie still be right? Would Krauss's efforts, even then, be considered, by and large, repulsive rather than heroic? Yes, it's a muddy realm of inquiry. All those hypotheticals. But it's precisely the hypotheticals that make the answer so obvious.

—*Kim*

July 10, 2019

Dear Knausgaard,

Do you like Edgar Allan Poe? I ask because your work often reminds me of his. Because underneath all those ordinary scenes of your sort of ordinary life—all those diapers and prawns and baby carriages and cigarettes and sausages and books and beers—there's some kind of flexible metaphysical web. This, in fact, is a big part of what attracts me to your work (and Poe's). Deep down, it's all so frontal-lobe.

Take, for instance, your central preoccupations (at least as I see them), which I listed a while back:

- the inner vs. the outer
- biological life vs. material reality
- freedom vs. responsibility
- the heart vs. the mind

What's interesting about these is how they're all of a type. I'm talking about all those *versus*. *Versuses?* In any case, they're striking. Unusual. But in fact, oppositional pairs constitute a special element of your work.

Do I misread you? I worry about it. But I don't think so. You spend so much time analyzing these dualities in *My

Struggle it would be hard to overstate their significance. It's a strange state of affairs, the way you spell out these fixations so often, at such length, in a project that's propelled above all by the goals of "openness" and "inexhaustibility," both terms that point to the desire to touch something beyond dualities, something absolute, infinite, sacred—something *real*. Or, to put it another way, terms that seem to promise contact with whatever it is that lies beyond the limiting constructs we humans rely upon so heavily in order to interpret the world around us. And yet, within this never-say-die project—this gigantic novel that essentially attempts to outrun itself and, in this way, to crack the code of inexhaustibility— you reiterate again and again the myriad ways in which inner experience differs from outer expression, and the way biological forms differ from inorganic ones, and the way freedom opposes individual responsibility, and the way the mind bickers more or less constantly with the blind, dumb heart. Not to mention—it occurs to me just now—the way the "masculine" (as you understand that quality) is so consistently at odds with what you deem the "feminine."

The tremendous energy you pour into this business of locking down exactly the same sorts of constructs you strive so earnestly, at precisely the same moment, to escape: it's funny. And sad. It's mission impossible! I suspect this accounts for the great feeling of affection I have for you (I mean, in this case, you as a person). Because the fact is, I love everybody's inner Quixote.

With warm regards,
K.

July 13, 2019

Dear Knausgaard,

The last book of *My Struggle* reminded me, as I know it did many others (the word crops up regularly in reviews), of an ouroboros, which is to say a snake that eats its own tail. Or, to be a little less classical about things, it reminded me of autophagy, plain and simple: self-cannibalism.

An ending that circles back to its beginning seems more or less inevitable in a novel about writing a novel, which is what the final installment of *My Struggle* explicitly is. How else could such a story—a story in which the hero's journey is made of sentences, paragraphs, and pages—possibly end but in a meta-collision between the act of writing and the narrative that's been written?

This is also how Proust closes *Remembrance of Things Past*, a novel likewise concerned, above all, with its own composition, which is to say, with the relationship of literature to life. Yet Proust's recursive gesture at the end of that novel has none of the claustrophobia of Book 6, none of the airlessness that Lisa and others have complained about so bitterly (Dwight Garner's review in the *New York Times* describes the 1,200-page brick of a book as a "life-drainer—so dense and dull that time and light seemed to bend around it"). Instead, Proust's finale evokes visions of "profound azure" and impressions of "coolness, of dazzling light," all characteristic, in his view, of the intoxicating sensation of vertigo that occurs when time is revealed, suddenly, to be nothing like the linear progression we usually conceive it to be—an arrow hurtling out of the present into the future and leaving, in its wake, the slipstream of the past—but instead something closer to an invisible, multi-dimensional environment, the dizzying strata of which are every so often illuminated through the act of remembering.

But Proust does more than simply describe this feeling of vertigo. And he does more than illustrate it. He actually summons the state in the reader by recalling the most famous scene in all of *Remembrance of Things Past*: that bit near the beginning in which, as an adult, Marcel tastes a morsel of madeleine cake soaked in tea and, as the flavor blooms in his mouth, finds himself suddenly transported back decades earlier to those occasions when, as a boy, he used to eat this same kind of cake dipped in his Aunt Leonie's favorite tisane while standing at her side. That scene, of course, announces the novel's major theme: the potency of memory, the slipperiness of time. But in referring to it again at the novel's close, and revealing that it was this very moment that inspired the composition of the novel we've almost come to the end of, Proust reveals the "madeleine moment" to be much more than simply a proclamation of thematic intent. It is, in fact, the seed that's grown the novel; the entire narrative has unfolded from it, opened up and extended through time (which is in this case physically represented by text—thousands of pages of it, pages filled with the most gorgeous imagery, elegant digressions, and sophisticated syntax), as if obeying the intricate codes of some kind of literary DNA. And because any reader who has made it through the 4,000-plus pages that stand between the first mention of the madeleine and the second has necessarily spent an enormous chunk of time with the novel—has, in fact, grown somewhat older in its presence—the memory of the madeleine no longer belongs to Proust alone, but to the reader as well. Which means that when reminded of that early scene so close to the novel's end, the reader experiences exactly what Proust set out to reveal: the way in which time is occasionally capable of skipping through itself, the way past and present can, every once in a while, overlap or even overtake one another, and transport us—briefly—into a shimmering state of suspension, a time outside of time, or perhaps wholly dissolved within it. In this way, that dainty, buttery, shell-shaped teacake becomes the tiny, almost invisible seam in the narrative Möbius strip that is *Remembrance of Things Past*. And so Proust's novel ends. It completes itself. And yet it is not, in the strictest sense of the word, *finished* because the novel as a whole exists, thanks to this literary sleight of hand, in a state of timelessness, just like its central metaphor. In other words, although clearly finite, *Remembrance of Things Past* forever gestures toward something unlimited and inexhaustible.

Needless to say, what you do is nowhere near so finely orchestrated. Not that anybody expected something like that from you. It's clear from the outset that *My Struggle* is a roughly hewn thing—that's part of its charm, and I wouldn't trade its lumbering gravitas for anything, even a better ending. But the novel does approach its own conclusion in a weirdly bullheaded way. Fevered yet full of calculation. Not in any sense straightforward, but at the same time simplistic.

Just as you do in Books 1-5, in Book 6 you tackle a discrete period of time: that span of years during which you wrote (and continue to write, for as long as the final volume lasts) *My Struggle*. Opening in September 2006, just as Book 1 is about to hit the stores, the narrative progresses more or less chronologically as you chomp your way along the spine of the next several years until—eventually, inevitably—the story catches up with itself, at which point the text proceeds in step with its own composition until the last line of the novel, in which you claim, with the same kind of solemnity a small child cooks up in order to announce they're about to run away from home, that you are "no longer a writer."

Typing it out, it doesn't sound so bad. It sounds kind of interesting. Clever at least. So why did I feel so spent by the end of the book? Was it simply a matter of length? Maybe. 1,200 pages is a long haul. Or did it have something to do with "The Name and the Number"—the gigantic essay on Hitler that entirely disrupts the narrative flow and takes up the middle third of the book? This, clearly, was a factor. Because thinking about the Holocaust is never not existentially unmanageable. But I don't think that's it either.

... continued (July 14)

I've spent the last few days actively avoiding the Hitler essay, though every so often, feeling diligent, I'd open up my wellworn advance reader's copy of the Archipelago edition of

Book 6, with its funky mustard-colored cover, flip to somewhere in the middle, take a reluctant nip of the text, flop the book shut (it makes a satisfying "thwap" sound), then pick up anything else at all—the bills, a new memoir by Naja Marie Aidt, a pencil, my cellphone, a peach.

"The Name and the Number" is a difficult read, above and beyond the depressing subject matter. It's dense, eccentric, elastic, wildly intelligent, and, at the same time, often in the same paragraph, fairly half-baked. It's also nearly impossible to summarize. Yes, it looks at the importance of names, in both literary and "real life" contexts, and at the idea of numbers, which is what you argue humans become when they are crowded into ghettos, factories, trains, and concentration camps, or lined up at the edges of pits and shot dead. And yes, through its analysis of *Mein Kampf* and other relevant texts, the essay composes a revealing psychological portrait of Hitler in his early years, humanizing him not in order to create a sympathetic character, but to prove that he was, after all, neither devil nor demon. He was one of us. A human being. It also analyzes the poetry of Paul Celan, in particular "The Straightening." And with this analysis, you enter the mystical realm of metalinguistics, where you laboriously parse the terms *I*, *you*, *it*, *we*, and *they* (which, in a Buberish mood, you deem "the fundamental elements of life"). The essay also describes the 2011 Norway terrorist attacks by Anders Behring Breivik, in which 77 people (most of them children) were murdered, and brings us around once more to one of your touchstones: the idea of utopia. Etymologically speaking, this word means "no place" or "not place," which, you suggest, is exactly where

Breivik and Hitler both spent their lives: in a not-place composed of ideology, ideas, and abstractions, a place completely divorced from the real, material world, the messy, imperfect world of concrete things and soft, specific people. "The Name and the Number" does all of this and still bristles with hundreds of digressions, both small and large, on everything from the death of myths, to the dehumanizing consequences of the Enlightenment, to the elusive nature of charisma, to name just a few. Basically, it's all over the fucking place.

But that's not what wiped me out. What wiped me out was how *symmetrical* everything got. Almost mathematical. It was all those oppositional pairs. You kept piling them on. "The Name and the Number," for instance, revolves, pretty self-evidently, around another one of these: the name vs. the number. Then there's the related, though not identical, individual vs. society—another way of saying "I" vs. "We." Ultimately all these pairs point to what is, for the purposes of *My Struggle*, the most important polarity of all: literature vs. ideology. I understood early on that this was a major preoccupation for you—you said something along these lines in Iceland—and yet it took me until about halfway through the Hitler essay to finally get it: you're trying to prove something. And nothing's more tiresome than someone trying to prove something.

*****

Just now (this is neither here nor there: I only thought you might be interested) there's a rabbit in our backyard stretched out in the overgrown grass beneath a dark green plastic stool, the top of which has faded from years of sun exposure. The rabbit alternately grooms its front paws and nibbles at the grass, but only the grass that's easily within its reach. Every once in a while the animal stops both of these activities to raise its head, and at these moments it appears actually incandescent as it allows the sunlight (which rakes under the seat of the stool at a low angle; it's 6:30 pm) to caress its back, its head and its ears, which rotate ever so slightly.

*****

When Book 6 finally emerges from the long aside that is "The Name and the Number" and resumes tracking your unfolding life, Linda is very ill. After an intense period of mania, she's entered a deep depression. You are at this point in the story already at work on Book 6. Book 5 is on the verge of publication. Linda has weathered the tsunami of fame that by now is old news for you, but it's taken a toll on her. As has the work itself, which reveals her to be weak and often selfish; beautiful and talented but at same time exhaustingly insecure; by turns demanding and doting. You expose her in ruthless detail over the course of the novel. And why do you force her to suffer such indignities? Because you have a goal. You want to write something "exceptional." You want to make the world "real" again through your writing (hey, God), which is why you try to "describe reality as it is," which entails describing it as it is for *you*, since "there is no other reality" (hey, Maturana). And to do this, you explain, to "really go there, you can't be considerate."

Toward the end of Book 6, you write that *My Struggle* has been a failed experiment but one not without value. In relaying the "exclusively everyday events" that you have, you insist that you haven't broken any new ground, and that the only truly unusual aspect of the novel resides in your use of real names, because these tie everything you've written to specific individuals. This is why you say that *My Struggle* "has hurt everyone around me, it has hurt me, and in a few years, when they are old enough to read it, it will hurt my children. If I had made it more painful, it would have been truer."

You write these lines on page 1007 of Book 6. On page 1088 you describe an interview Linda has with a psychiatrist who asks her to try to do something normal—just some small, ordinary task—in order to pull herself out of her depression. "I don't do anything," Linda whispers. This, of course, is what you've been telling your readers all along. It's you who does the shopping, you who cleans the house, you who cooks the dinners, you who picks up the kids from daycare, even as you crank out volume after volume of a magnificently idiosyncratic and physically gigantic novel. And all the while Linda, for her part, often seems to need a break from things. Nor can she quite manage to get her act together, work-wise.

*****

Many critics claim you lack craft, but they're wrong. You've got craft coming out of your ears. *A Time for Everything* makes that clear. But of course in *My Struggle* you've abandoned nearly all overt gestures of craft, and yet you still make interesting strategic choices, and these ultimately are a matter of craft, just a little harder to see. Often these choices have to do with sly juxtapositions: Linda sobbing in a public park, her shoulders shaking, as if something had "crashed inside her," while you, two pages later, note that you're able to write "with ease and focus." Or Linda opening and closing her mouth as if "gasping for air," while you, in the very next scene, parse the intricacies of the publicity plan for the launch of Book 5. Such juxtapositions make the selfishness of your project clear to everyone, including yourself, which is both admirable and crafty (in both senses of the word). Because your honesty at these moments, which indicates self-awareness and, at the same time, a muffled self-loathing, functions a little like a Get Out of Jail Free card. After all, it's all part of the story.

Toward the end of Book 6, the meta-elements of the novel grow very deep and a little obscene. Linda's in a psychiatric hospital, suicidal and suffering from something close to psychosis, and still you keep writing. You're a madman. You're obsessed. You know you're obsessed, but you can't stop writing. The reader knows you're obsessed, but they can't stop reading—even as each paragraph seems to squeeze a little more life out of Linda, whose illness spreads like a stain over the remaining pages of the novel.

> "Focused on truth, the writer ceases to be concerned with values. To observe and to search for truth thus becomes the writer's unique and ultimate ethics."
> —Gao Xingjian

It's gotten late, quarter to nine. Since 6:30, when I told you about the rabbit (yes, it's taken me that long to write two pages), we've had a dramatic thunderstorm. Now the air feels freaky—soupy but cool. Receding groans of thunder are audible in the distance. James is listening to a soccer match on his smartphone, lying on the couch with a heating pad under his spine. He threw out his back the other day and has been in a black mood as a result. I've been working outside on the porch but it's nearly dark now. So—

Signing off,
Kim

July 21, 2019

Dear Knausgaard,

I'm writing to you from Vermont. We drove up—James, Jonah, and I—yesterday in one-hundred-degree heat. We're staying at the ski house of some friends. It's on a mountain, so it's cooler and there's a good breeze. James and Jonah have gone fishing, but the plan, when they get back, is to spend the afternoon with Nina, who lives half an hour away, in Burlington, so we can celebrate Jonah's thirteenth birthday together. I would feel more nostalgic about the childhood my son is hurtling away from if I were the only one afflicted by that emotion, but last night he asked me to read him *Harry Potter*, which I used to do all the time, over and over again, when he was much younger. I was surprised but pleased by the request, and read from *The Chamber of Secrets* for about thirty minutes, until I noticed that he'd fallen asleep, just as he used to when he was little. Face down on the seat of an oversized armchair, his long legs were posting off the ottoman. It's hard growing up.

    I always have trouble sleeping when I travel and last night was no exception. First it was the over-fluffy pillow that wouldn't let me sleep, then it was the tiny black biting gnats, then the stillness of the air, then the mosquitoes, then the partiers in the apartment downstairs. Then it was James' snoring, which I try to remind myself to cherish. It's not that loud. It's him. Content, asleep. But that never works. I spent most of my time awake reading a book Lisa lent me last week called *Flash Count Diary*, by Darcey Steinke. It's about menopause, which Lisa's just starting to deal with and about which she, as a result, has many pressing questions. I relate and I don't. For me it began very early, right after Jonah was born, and all I can say is that I'm glad to be on the other side of it. When I think of the actual "change" itself—painful as it was, and it was—I think of the sound my computer makes when I empty the trash on my desktop. That quick, crinkly sound of something getting burned up. Disappearing. Since then, I sense death more than I did before. I smell it all the time, in fact—in flowers, in fresh fruit, in the part in children's hair. I hear it in birdsong. And every day I notice its tendrils rooting deeper into my own less and less graceful body. What can you do? Write a novel, I guess. That's one option. That's what you did. This is what I was thinking last night as I lay with Steinke's book over my sternum, looking up at the knotty pine plank ceiling.

Writing when you feel death at your heels means writing well, I've noticed. So why don't more people do it? Why don't I do it? It seems to me you can cultivate an awareness of death, which is the same thing as cultivating an awareness of life, or you can cower in fear and log on to Twitter. You can watch a junky movie. Read the news. Pick a fight. They're all so much easier.

Early in Book 1, you write a series of joke epitaphs for yourself. I found these charmless and not very funny, but I was also intrigued by what they seemed to signal, the idea that the entire novel was going to be, for you, a confrontation with your own mortality. Of course, each of us understands that we will die one day, though mostly we perceive this fact as just that—a fact, a more or less abstract certainty. We forget about it as easily as we forget about gravity or the air we breathe. But for 3,600 pages you never turn away from the inevitability of your own death, whenever or however it might arrive. This is what drove you to write so much, so quickly. Even when you're describing the intricacy of a lobster's shell. Or speaking "applish" to an apple for the amusement of your daughter. Or placing a frozen pizza on a tarnished—"mottled brown or, perhaps more exactly, blackened"—baking tray and sliding it into the oven for your children's dinner. Or noting the garish green make-up on your wife's eyelids when she comes home from the hospital for a weekend visit. You pay such close attention to life because you pay such close attention to death.

When we were in Maine last month, Julie (my friend, the composer, not Julie my sister-in-law) told me an interesting theory she'd come up with. She said she thought the reason you're able to pull the reader through such long, seemingly barren stretches of near-non-narrative, like the snow/beer/New Year's Eve party scene in Book 1, which she happened to be in the middle of reading at the time, is because your method of piling on details ("I went back up to the garage, replaced the shovel, found the four torches in the bag, lit them one by one in the dark, not without pleasure, for the flames were so gentle, and the blue in them rose and sank according to which way the current of air carried them...") is very much like what we all do when we tell each other stories about the most important events we've experienced—events that for one reason or another, took us by surprise or perhaps even threatened our lives or our understanding of the world.

"Take 9/11, for instance," said Julie. We were eating something terrible—a recipe she'd brought up involving black-eyed peas, spinach, and walnuts. Julie's super-thrifty. It was our third go at the gray leftovers. "I bet you remember exactly where you were when you found out about the Twin Towers, right?"

"Yes, I remember—I was in our apartment on Symphony Road. I'd just dropped Nina off at pre-school, and I'd been trying to reach my friend Beth for a long time but the line was busy. When I finally got through, it was her husband, Dan, who picked up."

"And I'm guessing you probably remember everything about the moment he told you what was happening. I mean your physical surroundings?"

"I do. The phone was dark green. It hung on the wall in the kitchen, near the dining room. It was the old-fashioned kind with a curly cord. And the cord didn't match the phone. It was black and too short. I had to stand near the wall because it didn't stretch."

"What else?"

"I can see the whole apartment—the upper floor, at least, all those windows. The sky was blue. No clouds. Not a wisp. I remember noticing that before I got on the phone. And I can still see the pinkish-beige linoleum peeling up in the back corner of the kitchen, near the stove. I remember looking at the gray keys on the phone, which were right at eye level, when Dan told me to turn on the TV."

"That's how it works. Ask anyone where they were on 9/11 when they found out, and they'll remember the tiniest details. I think that's how he creates the sense of suspense that keeps you going. You're waiting for some big moment to arrive."

Julie's so smart. That's exactly what you do. On the surface this seems like not much more than a cute trick, the world's longest shaggy dog story, because the life-changing event you're leading up to never arrives. It's just life. For now.

Best wishes,
K. A.

July 24, 2019

Dear Knausgaard,

Last summer we spent a week on the island in Maine with James' family. Fourteen people. I'm not asocial but that's a lot of people. I couldn't handle it so I hid out a good stretch of each day in a one-room cabin, which I'd arranged as a study. I'd brought up several books with me, including all of *My Struggle*, and one afternoon, as I sat at an almost child-sized desk near a window that looked out over a field of ferns, I leafed through all six volumes with the idea that I might jot down some of my thoughts regarding the novel as a whole. At one point my brother-in-law Sasha came by to give me a bottle of white ale and a plate of cheese and crackers. The ale was bitter and a little salty. I sipped at it as I continued to flip through the books in what I remember now as a curiously dizzying experience. There were so many tiny things embedded in so many big things in those pages. You as a kid holding your breath to drink a glass of warm, unpasteurized milk. You biking up hills with an early crush, hoping for a kiss that never arrives. Your mother making you wear a girl's swim cap to the public pool. Your father calling you "Kaklove." You kissing Linda for the first time, then fainting. You and Yngve getting drunk in Kristiansand with your grandmother at her kitchen table before your father's funeral. Blackened fish sticks on a griddle. Split sausages in cloudy water. Butter scraped onto a knife in a "schist-like" formation. Your father twisting your ear and screaming at you for losing a sock. You balancing potted flowers on your son's stroller. You pretending you spilled apple juice so your date wouldn't realize the wet spot on your underwear was semen. You talking with your mother about putting down the cat. You gazing at your newborn daughter, her eyes "like two black lamps," her movements "reptilian." You boiling prawns. You smoking cigarettes. You cutting your face with a broken beer bottle. Linda desperately weeping at the airport after her father's funeral. You pouring cornflakes. You changing diapers. You inserting the card-like key of a rental car into its slot. You taking a train in southern Sweden, staring at the red sun through a wall of white mist… Literally tens of thousands of details, even hundreds of thousands of them, flashed in front of my eyes as I let the pages fall from my hand and then let them fall again and again as I sipped the salty ale.

When I'd finally exhausted myself with this exercise, I headed up to the house to help make dinner. Julie was in the kitchen. I tried to act normal but we've known each other a long time.

"What's up?"

"I don't know. It's just the Knausgaard. Those books are so… Maybe it's also the beer Sasha gave me. I don't think I've ever had such strong beer." My eyes kept watering. I felt ridiculous.

"It's good to love a book that much," said Julie, giving my back a rub.

I wandered back outside to find James, who was standing near the grill checking his cell phone. He also asked me what was wrong. I told him that I'd just spent the last half hour leafing through *My Struggle*, crying.

"Why?"

"I don't know!"

"It's funny, but for all your talk about that novel, I can never tell if you like it or not."

"Of course I like it. It's amazing. I've never read anything like it. It's just ... there are no angles to it. No edges. And what's good about it is also what's bad about it. It's all mixed up. Like a person."

Kim Adrian

August 3, 2019

Dear Knausgaard,

I often wonder what that woman in Iceland—the one in the gray dress—saw when she looked at you that night you gave the keynote in Reykjavik. When I looked at you, I saw a tall, handsome man in the prime of his life. Or maybe just a couple of degrees past the prime of his life. But still vital, still virile. I saw a large man. I saw an earnest man. I saw an unsmiling man. And this, as I suspect you know, is precisely the kind of man most women, myself included, like to see smile. This is why I watched you carefully—to see if you would. When you finally did, just once during the question and answer period, I found you charming. Almost boyishly so. *Adorable*, actually, is the word that flashed across my mind. But I didn't entirely trust you. Neither did my daughter, who sent me a sidelong eye roll when you claimed to have read *thousands and thousands of books*. Lisa says I have a problem with trust, but that's not true. I just have good radar, and the sad fact is, a lot of people are untrustworthy; I simply pick up on it quicker than some. My radar's not infallible, however, and the night I saw you in Reykjavik it was jammed. I just couldn't get a good read on you. Maybe this was on account of the woman sitting next to me. I felt so bad for her.

It's very difficult, as I've mentioned, to keep you, Karl Ove Knausgaard, the world-famous author, separate from you, my imaginary friend KOK, separate from you, whoever you are, I mean the person behind the persona, the one I suspect I wouldn't like too much, the one I think I wouldn't trust. Your work, with its staunch refutation of "fiction," and total embrace of "reality," has everything to do with this confusion, this muddying of the lines. But by this point the confusion itself has attained a significance well outside the novel, outside the realm of literature, even. In fact, I've come to view it—the drastic blurring of the boundaries that distinguish you the author, you the character, and you the public persona—almost as a kind of performance art concerning the convoluted relationship between an artwork's subject, its critical reception, and the artist, him- or herself. I know you'd cringe at the thought. Performance art is hardly your cup of tea. But you have to admit, you've become something very interesting, both more and less than human: a little unreal. A fantasy. An ideal.

> "A writer should not allow himself to be turned into an institution."
> —Jean-Paul Sartre

Basically, you're a big old screen—perfect for all kinds of projections. But why? Why are you so perfect for projections? I have some thoughts on this score, but it's extremely hot again here today. My T-shirt's sticking to my back. I've drawn every shade in the apartment, yet irregular bars of sunlight still seep through the cracks to shimmer on the walls, and I have urgent plans for a nap.

... *continued (still groggy, still hot)*

I was wrong before when I said time doesn't count as a "thing" for you. It does. Because while it's true that Proust's shadow lies very long across *My Struggle*, you've still managed to do something really interesting with time, something different.

The story of the life that unfolds over the pages of *Remembrance of Things Past* is viewed, always, through the prism of memory. This Proust makes clear from the outset, with the madeleine incident. And in case we're tempted to forget it—to immerse ourselves in the narrative as if it were an account of Marcel's actual life unfolding, rather than his recollection of that life *as it has unfolded*— Proust reminds us by way of his voice, the tone of which is pitched, on every page, with retrospective distance. This is why so much of *Remembrance of Things Past* feels practically crystalline: intricate, sharp, clear. Because hindsight really is 20/20. But you—you plunge through each volume of *My Struggle* with all the dumbass myopia of the here and now, purposefully making yourself adopt the attitude and voice of the child/teenager/young man/lover/husband/father you happened to be when the main narrative of each book takes place. In other words, your ten-year-old self, in Book 3, *sounds* like a ten-year-old, and never like Proust's *memory* of his ten-year-old self:

> It was in vain that I lingered beside the hawthorns—inhaling, trying to fix in my mind (which did not know what to do with it), losing and recapturing their invisible and unchanging odour, absorbing myself in the rhythm which disposed their flowers here and there with the lightheartedness of youth and at intervals as unexpected as certain intervals in music—they went on offering me the same charm in inexhaustible profusion, but without letting me delve any more deeply, like those melodies which one can play a hundred times in succession without coming any nearer to their secret.

No, your ten-year-old self says things like:

> We used to have a shit in the forest when we were on our walks. We would climb up trees and shit from there, squat on top of a cliff and shit over the edge, or on the bank of a stream and shit in it. All to see what happened and how it felt. What color the turds were, whether they were black, green, brown, or light brown, how long and fat they were, and what happened when they lay there glistening on the forest floor, between heather and moss, whether there would be flies swarming around them or beetles climbing over them.

In Proust's novel we feel the distance between the *then* of the narrative and the *now* of its telling so keenly that time itself becomes a kind of character. In yours, we bumble through time, just as we do in real life. And yet, though you resist it, you are not immune to the occasional moment of retrospective wisdom, nor to memories, of course. At times, memories even open up within other memories within Proustishly expanded moments of the narrative present, as when, for example, in Book 2, you smoke a cigarette on your apartment balcony in Malmö and sip a glass of flat soda as you bring the reader back to that time, two years earlier, when you fell in love with Linda, and then back further still, to the time you first met and were rejected by her, and then forward again to her pregnancy and the birth of your first child, and on and on—in fact it's a full 467 pages until you finally stub out your cigarette and take your last sip of soda before heading back inside.

But mostly it's your treatment of time as a constant rush—a rush within which memory naturally, reliably, blooms again and again—that justifies all those pages. Because the length of *My Struggle* is not simply the priapic expression of an outsized male ego that it appears to be at first (and second and third) blush, but instead represents a real excursion, not so much through time, as through you. The result is a nearly holographic—or, better yet, a hololinguistic, or, still better, I think, an almost holotemporal—portrait of a single human being. And perhaps it was this that the woman in the gray dress saw that night as she gazed at you, wearing an expression that looked, at least from where I was sitting, a lot like religious ecstasy. Yes, to her, you were not, I suspect, simply a man standing at a podium giving a pretty good reading, but father, son, husband, lover, and child all at once.

Or, who knows, maybe she was just crushing on you. It's really impossible to say.

—K. A.

August 22, 2019, 1:22 a.m.

Dear Knausgaard,

The air is crazy still tonight. Dead still. I can't sleep. Normally I'd read but I'm in the middle of *Malina*, by Ingeborg Bachman, and tonight, when even the crickets sound suicidal, it's just not an option. So I've come downstairs and opened up my laptop. I figure, why not write to KOK? Compared to Bachmann, you're a positive ray of sunshine.

I can't remember if you mention Ingeborg Bachmann at any point in Book 6, though you spend a lot of time writing about her lover, Paul Celan, whose poetry is one of the lynchpins of your Hitler essay. Have you read *Malina*? I'm not sure what I think of it yet, though I'm nearly done. I only know that something very strange happens with language in that book. Something not dissimilar to what happens in a Celan poem. It's as if meaning evaporates right off the words just as my eyes pass over them. That's almost surely the point, but I can't say I like it.

The narrator-protagonist of *Malina* is an unnamed woman who keeps trying to write things—letters, a book dedicated to one of her lovers, a fairy tale in her own head—but without success. Forget about writing, she can hardly think straight. It's the drugs—she takes a lot of them. Though clearly there are important metaphorical implications hovering around this inability.

Malina is a kind of ghost story in the sense that the narrator is haunted to the point of madness by memories of World War II and, more than that, by something harder to pinpoint, something she lost—or perhaps never had—simply because of her sex. Because to be a woman, according to this novel, is to be entirely without boundaries. This is what makes the narrator's language so hard to grasp. Every sentence floats, barely connected to its neighbors. The same is true of every image, every scene, and every line of dialogue. For an example of the kind of broken thought-syntax that fills *Malina*, consider this bit, from the long nightmare section in the middle third of the book:

> Now my father has my mother's face as well. It's an old, gigantic, washed-out face, in which the crocodile eyes may still be seen, but the mouth resembles the mouth of an old woman, and I don't know whether he is she or she is he, but I have to speak to my father, probably for the first time. Sire!

It's hard to make head or tail. Certainly Bachmann meant this to be the case, but I get impatient. I mean, come on, Inge, or whoever you are, take heart. Buck up. But the narrator of Bachmann's novel refuses to do anything, and bucking up is hardly in the realm of possibility because how can you buck up—against what can you shore yourself—if there's no *you* clearly distinguished from *me*, or *they*, or *it*, or (especially in this novel) an endless array of *hims*? In any case, the narrator's passivity is actually a kind of power. Her only one, since it's only by means of this passivity that she's able to expose her total lack of boundaries, which is to say, the truth of her existence.

It's interesting to think about *Malina* in relation to your work. Bachmann's exploration of boundarylessness stands in stark contrast to your obsession with the inner and the outer, which of course necessitates clear and plentiful and more or less rigid boundaries. But such things simply don't exist for Bachmann's protagonist. And maybe she's right. Maybe women really do lack the kinds of definitive boundaries you're so fond of, the kind absolutely necessary for an inner life as clearly distinct from an outer one. Physiologically, it's true, of course, that our boundaries are simply more breachable, for lack of a better word, than men's. And that knowledge alone takes its toll. *Malina* suggests that a woman's boundaries are erased first through the act of rape, and then merely (though just as effectively) through the thought of it. Her point, I think, is that it's not only individual men who destroy women's boundaries, but also, and more detrimentally, the vaguer, more impersonal, deeper, and generally self-regulating violence of that system we call patriarchy.

> "La femme n'existe pas."
> —Jacques Lacan

... *continued (9:15 am, with toast)*

Well, that was a terrible night's sleep. But the sun's up now and bouncing around the apartment, playing over our walls and bookshelves, filtered through the shadows of the leaves fluttering on the trees in our yard: hundreds of silent, rapidly moving splotches of light here and there, on the table, my hands.

All last night I kept trying to remember something you said somewhere in Book 6—some snarky anti-PC thing about gender-neutral language as it's currently practiced in Sweden. It was driving me nuts. I promised myself to find that passage in the morning, and thankfully, just now, I did. About two-hundred-and-fifty pages in, you write:

> Since *han* and *hun* are denotative of gender, it was suggested a new pronoun, *hen*, be used to cover both. The ideal human being was a gender-neutral *hen* whose foremost task in life was to avoid oppressing any religion or culture by preferring their own. Such total self-obliteration, aggressive in its insistence on leveling out, though in its own view tolerant, was a phenomenon of the cultural middle class, that segment of the population which controlled the media, the schools and other major institutions of society, and it existed, as far as I could tell, only in northern Europe.

I know it's part of your larger point—your fixation on the local—but sometimes your parochialism is astonishing. Though I suppose by now you've figured out that this kind of gender investigation has actually been taking place all over the world, in greater or lesser secrecy, in larger or smaller pockets, depending on the level of ambient oppression. Certainly, here in the U.S., gender-neutral language has gained significant ground, at least in the more liberal regions, where the pronouns "they" and "them" are often used to replace the binary terms "he" and "she" and "him" and "her."

You call the pronoun *hen*, and the philosophy behind it, "hostile to all difference," a condemnation of the highest order coming from you, since it's only in the differences between things that "reality's chunky solidity," as you put it, finds purchase. Indeed, you perceive in this little word a dangerous utopian impulse, a reaching toward homogenization, sameness, and de-individuation, not essentially different from the ideological impulses that inspired the Nazis—impulses you parse very carefully in "The Name and the Number." I understand what you're saying. I see what you're getting at. But in this case I think you've got it backwards. Because gender-neutral language isn't about embracing ideology at the expense of the individual, it's about extracting the individual from the flattening, homogenizing, de-individuating effects of non-gender-neutral language. Because there's plenty of ideology already there, obviously, embedded in that language.

Though to be perfectly honest, I, too, used to hate this kind of thing. I just found it incredibly antagonistic. All those *theys*—they were trying to change the way I speak! It pissed me off. But then I got it: *they're trying to change the way I speak*. They're disrupting one of the deepest, most basic structures of grammar and, by extension, thought itself. Why? Because, as I just said, language is inextricably bound up with ideology; it's stuck in it, growing out of it, and re-mixing back into it all the time. And one of the primary ideologies in which language is embedded is patriarchy. You might not want to change that—why should you? It works quite well for you. But consider *Malina*, and the way Bachmann breaks down sentences and thoughts before they cohere. This is not an artistic choice; it's a reflection of things as they are, language as it is—for her. That Bachmann's work is viewed as remarkable for these reasons isn't because of her craft. Indeed, I think it's fair to say that she rejected craft and style even more vehemently than you have. What to some might look like "style" in that novel is actually nothing more than a reflection of the fact that *Malina* is work made without compromise. If Bachmann had buckled, even a little, and made a linguistic concession here or there, if she'd allowed her narrator just a couple of boundaries—if only for plot's sake, if she'd fudged the truths she was tackling in order to fit them more comfortably inside the language she was using, there'd be no *Malina* to speak of.

Contrast that with the way you use language almost as if it were truly capable of something like "naturalness" or neutrality. Which I suppose it is—for you. But you're a man. White. Cis. Middle class. And these things all make a difference. Because language is, in itself, hardly a neutral medium. It's just that some people are able to use it in a way that contextually manages to behave in a more or less neutral manner.

In the middle of *Malina*, the narrator dreams she's been jailed because her incestuous father doesn't want her to spill the beans on his grotesque sins. The irony is that, while it's true she's desperate to write, what she wants to write has nothing to do with him. She wants to "write the sentence from the ground up." That she can't do so because of the lack of paper in her cell drives her mad. Without paper, she refuses to eat or drink, but as she begins to waste away, sentences form in the air around her. At one point the father spies on her through a peephole because he'd like to "copy" these words and take them from her. But she refuses to give voice to these airborne sentences, which "rejoice" around her. So determined is she to keep her father from stealing her words that she holds her breath and begins to die. "My tongue is dangling far out, but it does not reveal a single word."

I sometimes wonder if it's possible that you—who are not only (like Bachmann) a remarkable writer, but who also (unlike Bachmann) happen to fulfill society's deepest fantasies about what it means to *be* a writer, a "real" writer, a writer V. S. Naipaul would read, a writer Javier Cercas would think to include in his book—have been able to write about the domestic as you have and to elevate it to the realm of full-fledged literature precisely because you're a man, when hundreds, if not thousands, of women have been writing about these same realms, these same things—the diapers, the TV cartoons, the naps, the bath times, the dinner times, the snatched moments at the desk times, the strollers, the dirty dishes, the births, the pregnancies, the small hands on one's neck, the small mouth at one's ear, the marital stress, the parental ghosts—for god knows how long, and yet all those efforts have almost without exception been relegated to the dainty, dismissible ghetto of "women's writing." Was my sister-in-law right when she said that no woman could even have attempted something similar to what you've done because we're trained—through our upbringings and the daily deluge of media imagery depicting our sex as glossy, accommodating dipshits, not to mention the patriarchal agendas hidden in every aspect of social life, including the very structures of language itself—to limit ourselves, to keep ourselves slight, inconsequential, negligible? The choices for women, it seems, are two. Exactly this: stay in our ghetto; or suffer the kinds of consequences Bachmann enumerates in *Malina*. At least barring some major change. But who knows—maybe something *will* change.

> "A day will come when all women will have redgolden eyes, redgolden hair, and the poetry of their sex, their lineage, shall be recreated."
> —Ingeborg Bachmann

Wouldn't that be something?

Yay for they!
Kim Adrian

September 3, 2019

Dear Knausgaard,

Once, in my late twenties, I wrote a novel that never saw the light of day. I called it "Ink." It was about a man reading a book and the woman writing it and the conflicting desires they each had for the direction of the narrative. I thought I was writing a book about the special kind of communion that's sometimes possible through the medium of text.

> "Literature is love."
> —Vladimir Nabokov

But really I was doing something else. I was avoiding something. Myself, I think it's fair to say. Not that I didn't try to write something genuine, something with substance, with heft. I did. I even spent a stretch of weeks roaming around San Francisco, where James and I lived at the time, looking for a real live model for my male protagonist (whom I never named). I searched everywhere. Could that slender, German-looking man with the wire-rimmed glasses be him? No. What about that gimlet-eyed construction worker with the crazy red cheeks and silver hair? Or the skinny old man in the donut shop wearing the fedora and the brown suit with the shiny lapels? No, no. I looked for him every day as I walked around the city. Finally I found him on California Street boarding a bus near the intersection with Polk. He was very tall and a little hunched, dusky skinned with a prominent belly. Dark eyes. And black hair that fell in slightly greasy ringlets around his face, which was handsome in a complicated way, but not self-consciously so. I saw him for only a few seconds before the bus took off, leaving behind a hot cloud of exhaust. I can't abide exhaust, but I didn't budge as the airborne swill washed over me, so intent was I on scribbling down every detail I could remember about the man I'd just seen—all of it went into my little blue-covered spiral notebook as the bus hurtled away.

I'd been struggling for months to get my novel off the ground, but after that day I began to write in earnest. Even so, it took me a long time to finish, considering the slenderness of the final product. Three years! At the time, I didn't know why it was taking me so long, but now I have a theory: it's a lot harder, not to mention way more time-consuming, to avoid something than it is to simply confront it. In any case, about a month or so after I'd finally finished the novel, I was standing on line at a grocery store just a few blocks away from where I'd seen the tall, dark-haired man get onto the bus. As I waited for my turn to pay (what I was buying I no longer recall, I only know that I was anxious about money), I noticed a man one line over who looked very much like the man in my novel. Was it the same man I'd seen getting onto the bus three years earlier? I couldn't say. The process of turning him into a character had certainly distorted my memory of him—probably a lot. Only this much was clear: the man at the next register was of the same type: tall, big-boned, bearded, with black hair and a belly.

I walked home slowly, uphill, thinking, as the handles of the plastic bags full of groceries cut into my hands. James and I lived at the top of Russian Hill. I took an unusual route that day, up Green Street, which was always a little deserted. By the time I reached Larkin, a distinct feeling of unease had come over me. I had the sense that someone was following me, and when I turned to check, I saw the man from the grocery store. He, too, was walking up Green Street. How strange. Our apartment was still five blocks away, but every time I crossed another street, and turned to check if he was still there, he was—always at a distance of about half a block. By the time I reached our apartment I was truly frightened. I ran inside and up the stairs (we lived on the second floor), and, carefully avoiding the bay window in the living room, went straight into the bedroom, where the shades were drawn. I pulled one of these just an inch to the side and looked out. The man from the grocery store was standing across the street, leaning on a fire hydrant. Can you guess what he was doing?

Try.

Okay, I'll tell you. He was writing in a notebook.

This sounds like a fable, but it isn't. It's just an interesting thing that transpired. Was the man a serial killer, taking notes for his next murder, as I feared at the time? Or was he a city planner interested in the many unusual features of our intersection, with its steeply pitched sidewalks and wide views of both of the city's bridges? Was he—as I had once been—a writer thrilled to have finally found the model for the protagonist of his next novel? Or was he my own character from my own novel come to turn the tables on me? That, of course, is the only alternative that's clearly impossible. Obviously. And yet deep down, it is my favorite option, and the one I choose to believe.

I tell you this story because of something I once heard you say in an interview: "Every novel is a utopia." Something like that. I jotted it down, though really I had no clue what you meant. But now I think I get it. Every novel is a utopia—a "not place"—because how couldn't it be? A novel is a book, after all. And we enter books with our minds, not our bodies. We don't go anywhere to get into them, which is why it delights me to think that the man who followed me home that day in San Francisco might have been the protagonist of my own novel—because it's such a wonderful bit of magic when the life of the mind suddenly merges with the experience of the body. In fact, this is one of the great draws of *My Struggle*, one of the things its admirers admire so much: the way your descriptions seem to amplify the act of perception itself. The way the novel feels almost as if it had been torn from the very substance of your life, actually made *of* it. Which makes for a curiously porous reading experience. Even now—long after having finished Book 6—I am reminded at surprisingly frequent intervals of your project and remain, on a daily basis, inspired by your determination to "make the world real again" simply by paying attention to it.

And yet that bastard, Cercas, was right. The blind spot of a novel, a good novel, is by its very nature elusive. It not only poses an impossibility, it constitutes one. Which means that while *My Struggle* may *feel* like real life, and be *about* real life, it is, in the final analysis, merely a linguistic construction: a set of six fairly hefty books made of paper and some ink.

... continued (after an extended interlude with a box of almond tuile cookies)

Then again, nothing is ever truly black-and-white, cut-and-dry, this-or-that. For instance, real life obviously includes linguistic constructions. And linguistic constructions often—don't ask me how—include bits and pieces of real life. And a blind spot can be, at the same time, a searing point of focus.

In Book 6 you write: "The heart cannot reason. The brain does that. And if there was one thing I had learned in life, it was that the heart is everything, the brain nothing."

You often pit emotions against ideas, as if one were the inverse of the other. Boil *My Struggle* down to its essence (a hopeless task, granted) and this would more or less be what's left: a championing of emotion over intellect, an elevation of the mute and stubborn operations of the heart—which include not only feelings, but also the force of life itself—over the more subtle and sterile operations of the brain. But in reality, there's wide and messy overlap between the heart and the brain. From some angles, I'd even go so far as to say that they're essentially the same thing. We are not layer cakes, after all. Not stacks of ascending and descending values of awareness and engagement: consciousness/thought/feeling/emotion. Ideas are often very emotional. And at the root of many an emotion lurks an idea. Personally, I find this sort of muddling exciting. I suppose, for me, it constitutes freedom of a sort—not so much of expression as of *impression*.

*****

In your book *Autumn*, under the entry "The Migration of Birds," you describe taking a bag of garbage from the kitchen of your new house in Glemmingebro to the bin outside. Before heading back indoors, you stand still for a moment, in the drizzle, and gaze up at a flock of geese flying overhead. Inside again, you make dinner, tending the sausages (which have "developed a brownish-black crust") and the macaroni (swirling in "eddies of seething water"), while contemplating how a Platonic ideal—or something like it—takes up residence in the mind:

> Within me the migrating birds are living a life of their own. I'm not thinking of them, but they are there, in the stream of sensations and feelings which at times freeze into images. Not clear and distinct images, as with photographs, for that isn't how the external gets depicted within us, but as if in rifts: a few black triangles, a sky, and then that sound, of several pairs of wings beating up in the air.

Refining this thought a bit, you tack it carefully onto your central preoccupation—the sovereignty of immediate sensory perception and its constant companion, emotion—by explaining that the sound of birds flying overhead roused feelings in you: "What kind of feelings? I ask myself now, as

I write this. I know them so well, but only as feelings, not as thoughts or concepts." These lines are written in the present tense ("I ask myself now"), but at precisely the same moment (that's to say, in precisely the same text, the same paragraph) you locate yourself within that other moment, the one in the kitchen, as you pour the macaroni (also in the present tense) into a colander.

At this point in your musings, a memory of childhood intrudes and you write briefly about how, when you were very young, the world seemed boundless and full of possibility. But then, slowly, over time, you began to understand that in fact the world is finite, as the migration of birds, you argue, proves. For although they fly north and south, depending on the season, neither the place they leave, nor the place they fly toward is "abstract." Both, instead, are "concrete and local." You go on: "This is what I sensed as I wedged the spatula under the slices of sausage and placed them on the green serving dish, then poured the macaroni into a glass bowl. The world is material. We are always in a certain place. Now I am here."

But which "here" do you mean? The one that finds you putting sausages on a green dish, macaroni in a glass bowl? Or the one in which you actually wrote those lines, when you typed the words "Now I am here." At that moment, you were presumably sitting in front of your computer, just as I am sitting in front of my computer right now, at this very moment, which already is no longer this very moment. For instance, I am now typing different words. I can hear Jonah in the kitchen eating toast or cereal—something crunchy— and shifting his weight in the chair. It creaks. It's raining here, too, lightly but insistently: thousands of drops gently percuss our roof. It's strange: here I sit, at my desk, in my home, in a large, affluent, self-satisfied suburb just outside of Boston, but every time I glance at page 144, I am in your kitchen in Glemmingebro where it is also a gray, damp, drizzly day. And that—feels boundless.

With all my best,
Kim Adrian

Dear Knausgaard
By Kim Adrian

First published in this edition by Boiler House Press, 2022
Part of UEA Publishing Project
Copyright © Kim Adrian, 2022

The right of Kim Adrian to be identified as the Author of this work has been asserted by them in accordance with the Copyright, Design & Patents Act, 1988.

Cover Design and Typesetting by Louise Aspinall
Typeset in Arnhem Pro
Printed by Tallinn Book Printers
Distributed by NBN International

Editorial Coordination by James Hatton

Proofreading by Clare Kernie

This book is sold subject to the condition that it shall not, by way of trade or otherwise, be lent, resold, hired out, stored in a retrieval system, or otherwise circulated without the publisher's prior consent in any form of binding or cover other than that in which it is published and without a similar condition including this condition being imposed on the subsequent purchaser.

ISBN: 978-1-913861-38-4